The Untime

Hugh Ashton moved to Japan from the UK in 1988. He lives in Kamakura, a little to the south of Tokyo, with his wife Yoshiko. He is the author of many Sherlock Holmes mysteries, and various other works of fiction and non-fiction.

Other books by Hugh Ashton published by Inknbeans Press include:

Tales from the Deed Box of John H. Watson MD
More from the Deed Box of John H. Watson MD
Secrets from the Deed Box of John H. Watson MD
The Darlington Substitution
The Trepoff Murder
Notes from the Dispatch-Box of John H. Watson MD
Further Notes from the Dispatch-Box of John H. Watson MD
The Death of Cardinal Tosca
Without my Boswell
The Last Notes from the Dispatch-Box of John H. Watson MD

Tales of Old Japanese
At the Sharpe End

Sherlock Ferret and the Missing Necklace
Sherlock Ferret and the Multiplying Masterpieces
Sherlock Ferret and the Poisoned Pond
The Adventures of Sherlock Ferret

The Untime

A Novel of 19th Century Paris

by

Hugh Ashton

(Author of the Deed Box and Dispatch-box
series of Sherlock Holmes Adventures)

Inknbeans Press, Murietta, USA

The Untime : A Novel of 19th Century Paris

Hugh Ashton

ISBN-10: 0-692-34914-6
ISBN-13: 978-0692349144

Published by Inknbeans Press, 2014

This is a work of fiction. Names, characters, places, brands, media, and incidents are either the product of the author's imagination or are written in respectful tribute to the creator of the principal characters.

Body set in 11pt Didot, titles and headings in Bocklin

Book design and layout by j-views

www.inknbeans.com

www.TheUntime.info

Inknbeans Press,
25060 Hancock Avenue Bldg 103 Suite 458,
Murrieta CA 92562, USA

Dedication

To HILARY, who explored the Untime with me.

"WHAT THEN IS TIME? If no one asks me, I know what it is. If I wish to explain it to him who asks, I do not know."

Augustine of Hippo, *Confessions*

Contents

Foreword
by John Paul Catton

W HAT Ashton is particularly good at is to invent universes that are based on fictional creations we've seen before, but given original twists. He did it with the Sherlock Holmes canon, and now he's done it again with H.G. Wells. *The Untime* is a monstrous fountain of invention, a fictional universe based on Wellsian scientific romances and incorporating elements of Jules Verne, H.G. Wells, H.P. Lovecraft, Arthur Machen, and Frank Belknap Long.

Despite its short length, being the length of a novelette, the tale has a sprawling, epic quality that could hardly have been produced in any other fashion. It accurately captures the writing of that historical era. It's a style that becomes intriguing, then engaging, then enthralling. *The Untime* is rooted in its era and incredibly well-researched – but it also stretches the late Victorian scientific paradigm, dropping the names of all sorts of theories that belong to quantum physics at a time before quantum physics had been conceived, and so fleshing out a relatively slight plot with all manner of scientific concepts, speculations and discussions.

Despite all these intriguing concepts, it is the strong leading and peripheral characters that drive the densely written story, and provide the best shocks and twists. What is really shocking is how little the antagonist actually appears. In most stories this would be a problem, but here, because of the nature of the story, the threat to the time-space continuum

posed by Professor Rémy Lamartine becomes more
sinister, as he has the power to appear and strike at
any place, any time. The portrayal of the protagonist Jules Gauthier is
linked with the concept of the entire story; he is an
everyman, an observer thrown into a situation beyond his understanding, and as such serves as the
reader's viewpoint, as was common in the scientific
romances of the time. The most intriguing character
is probably Agathe Lamartine, who plays the role of
the daughter of the – quite literally – mad scientist.
At first she seems an 19th century damsel in distress,
but turns out to be more than capable of taking care
of herself. There is also Professor Schneider from
the Sorbonne, an academic rival of Lamartine's, who
seems a typical sceptic at first, but becomes a mentor
and staunch supporter of Gauthier's mission as the
plot unfolds.

A lot goes on that I cannot really discuss because
of spoilers, and that gives you a clue as to *The Untime*'s
scale and depth. The plot begins when journalist
Jules Gauthier makes the acquaintance of Professor
Rémy Lamartine, and becomes the audience to the
professor's theories on time, reality and the existence
of other dimensions. On a visit to Lamartine's house,
Gauthier is invited to inspect the machine that the
professor has constructed, and together the two venture into the Untime – the nebulous dimension that
exists outside of our reality and encompasses all of
time and space. The two time travelers return – but
Lamartine seems strangely changed by the experience, and over the days that follow his behavior becomes increasingly bizarre and erratic. Gauthier sus-
pects that Lamartine has become a danger to those
around him . . . and he's right. Lamartine, however,

poses a threat not only to Gauthier and his own family, but also to the continued existence of the perceived consensus reality that we call 'our world'.

One of the delights of this book is the amount of fascinating scientific concepts packed in, blurred into the fiction with invisible ease. It's worth commenting on Ashton's skill in narrative construction considering the difficulty of constructing plausible time paradoxes that don't hopelessly confuse the reader. The Lovecraftian elements, while not entirely unexpected, are extremely well done and a vivid depiction of cosmic horror. These sections achieve a very chilling feel; the atmosphere is shockingly effective at times.

The 19th century French settings are extremely well evoked, and despite the fantastical nature of the majority of the events, a feeling of realism is brought across to the reader. The historical "age" of the story is made much more concrete by creating the story in this manner. The book is able to play with the concepts of paradox and the vastness of eternity, but it doesn't allow itself to become confusing.

A beautifully written piece, then, with a superbly characterized cast and a hugely satisfying ending. An astonishing book, powered by symbolism and striking imagery, and wrapped up in bold, experimental narration. Looking over the Steampunk/Alternative History range as a whole there are few books that have this much impact, or that break the rules with such verve and distinction.

John Paul Catton is the author of *Tales From Beyond Tomorrow!*, *Moonlight, Murder & Machinery*, and the YA trilogy *Sword, Mirror, Jewel*.

Acknowledgements

As always, I want to thank other people who have made this book possible. Only one name appears on the cover, but a book is always the fruit of more than one person's labours.

First and foremost, Yoshiko, who has had to cope with the perils of the Untime while this book has been written.

Next, all who have commented and made suggestions regarding the story and its development. I have not always adopted these ideas, but they have all provided stimulation and inspiration.

John Paul Catton, for his unduly (in my opinion) flattering Foreword and evaluation of my work. Coming from another writer whose work I greatly admire, this is praise indeed.

And Jo at Inknbeans, who has continued to be more than an editor and publisher – she has become a true guide, philosopher, and friend, who has generously given her time and support to me during the (un)time while I have been writing this.

The Untime

Introduction

THE events I am about to describe may seem preposterous and incredible to some, but you may be assured of their veracity. Though I did not take detailed notes of all the conversations and activities recorded here, my relation of them is, to the best of my recollection, accurate.

I am supported in this assertion by my wife, Agathe Gauthier (*née* Lamartine), who was present at many of the events described here, and has been able to refresh my memory regarding many of them.

However, notwithstanding the truth of what I am setting down, I feel it inadvisable to make these facts public at this stage. I admit that the commotion and concern in the popular press surrounding the reported death of Professor Lamartine, who up to that time had occupied a prominent position in the public eye, tempted me at the time to give an open account of the savant's actions, but wiser counsels than mine prevailed.

I have therefore prepared this manuscript, and

propose that it be kept in some safe place, unopened until such time as I, and all connected with the events described here, have passed from this life. It may be that at some time in the future, eyes, as yet unknown to me, will discover and read these words, which will finally put an end to the mystery surrounding the Lamartine Affair, as it was then known.

Jules Gauthier
Paris, 1905

Chapter I

IT was a fine spring day in 189– when I visited my friend, the famous Professor Rémy Lamartine, at his laboratory in the suburbs of Paris. Lamartine had resigned his Chair at the University at some years ago, following a disagreement with a colleague as to who should have pre-eminence; the Professor of Greek Poetry, or the Professor of Astronomical Science. Lamartine himself, though a leading member of the department of physics, with an international reputation in that field, held that the classical scholar should precede the scientist, as the art of poetry had preceded the science of astronomy in the history of ideas.

However, there were those within the Regents of the University who disagreed with Lamartine, and he with them, to such a degree of violence that he was forced to step down from his post, and conduct such researches as he pleased as a private individual, while retaining the title of "Professor", to which, some who were opposed to him argued, he was not fully entitled as no longer being connected with the University.

I might add that this release from Academia was not a particularly onerous restriction upon him, financially or in any other way. Lamartine had married a wealthy woman, and her family's wealth would have enabled him to live on a luxurious scale, should he have a wish to do so. As it happened, his cupidity was directed only towards knowledge, and the money that might have been spent on frivolous gewgaws and knick-knacks was instead spent on mysterious apparatuses and the materials needed to construct them, as well as the generous salaries with which he rewarded his loyal assistants.

The house which contained his laboratories was a large one, and had formerly been the family residence of his wife's family. He now occupied it through right of inheritance, and, standing in its own extensive grounds, it was perfectly located as regards his neighbours, who were seldom inconvenienced by the noises, fumes, and occasional small explosions that proceeded from the rear outbuildings where the practical portions of the experiments took place.

I had come to know Professor Lamartine through our mutual membership of a musical society, which sold subscriptions to concerts. I had myself subscribed, as one of the promised concerts was to give us Johann Sebastian Bach's Goldberg Variations, which comprise some of my favourite pieces of music. At the concert, which took place about a year before the events related in this story, I discovered myself seated next to a man of advanced middle age, with a shock of black wiry hair, and a short beard, clad in evening dress which showed that the wearer had enjoyed many dinners in it, if the stains thereupon were any guide.

To my astonishment, before the recital started, my neighbour produced a large pad of artist's sketching paper and a roll of coloured pencils. As the music started, he began drawing, and my astonishment increased when I saw he was producing a visual representation of the themes and development of the variations, from the first Air, through the Variations, to the final Quodlibet and the reprise of the Air. All this was done almost as a mathematical graph, but one which acted as a perfect guide to the music.

Though what he had produced was far from being standard musical notation, and a musician would be unable to play the exact notes from his drawing, what I beheld on the paper, to my mind, completely captured the complexity of Bach's thoughts as expressed in the music.

I said as much to my companion, and he appeared pleased.

"You think so? Well, I am glad to hear you say that. This is an idea that came to me only this morning, and I fear it needs more thought and rigour before I can call myself pleased with it. However, not a bad start, though I say it myself. I am pleased to discover that you appreciate the theory behind the imperfect practice. Maybe you will join me at my club for a drink after this concert?"

I was later to discover that this was a typical utterance of Lamartine. Whatever work he was engaged upon never seemed to be exactly as he wanted it to be. His mind built up the most elaborate edifices, many of which were doomed to failure even before the first attempt was made to put them into practice, and many more of which had to be abandoned part-

way through their implementation. However, such
failures were hardly ever the result of a lack of rigour or precision on the part of their inventor. Rather, the thoughts behind them were of so advanced
and complex a nature that our present age lacks the
means to put them into practice.

I have heard Lamartine expound for some time,
for example, on the method by which men could be
sent to the Moon, and then return. Every step of the
process that he explained was perfectly sound, but
with our present abilities in the field of manufactur-
ing, for example, we could never produce the kind of
machinery that he described.

"Nor is that all, my dear Gauthier," he added. "To
reach the Moon, to land safely upon it, and then return to our Earth, requires the kind of calculations
that would tax even the Analytical Engine designed
by the Englishman Charles Babbage and never completed. Before we could even think of launching our
craft into the æther, we would need reams of paper
and forests of pencils to determine the exact date
and time, to the very second, when the voyage should
begin. And that process would have to be repeated
for every significant event on the voyage. Some day,
perhaps, a new Babbage will invent a machine that
will perform these calculations."

"Not you?" I asked.

Lamartine shook his head. "The design and construction of such a machine, though complex, would
be tedious in the extreme. It is a matter for a me-
chanic, or an engineer, not a scientist. Though I ap-
plaud Babbage's efforts, I cannot help but consider
that his talents would have been better spent in another direction."

"So we will never reach the Moon because of our

inability to perform the calculations that will take us there?"

"That is merely one of the factors which may impede our efforts. Another is the lack of suitable materials. Even my primitive calculations show that the steel we now use would be too heavy, and there is not enough aluminium in the world to construct such a vehicle. We must await the development of suitable metals. It is sad," he sighed. "When I was a lad, I had dreams that Man might fly to the Moon. Perhaps I would not be the very first, I felt, but I might be among the first men to travel to another world. But it is not to be. The task is too much for one man, and will require the resources of a whole government."

"And no government is interested in such a thing, of course."

Lamartine laughed bitterly. "They are interested in explosives and armour plate, faster ships, and longer ranges for their guns. If the Moon were a naval coaling station, our government, as well as those of the British and Germans, would be racing to get there. But as it is..." His voice tailed off and he took a sip of his cognac.

We held many conversations following the concert. He speedily discovered that I am a journalist, writing regularly for one of the more serious weekly magazines, and he was kind enough to act as my advisor when I was asked by my editors to write on scientific subjects. Not only did he most generously provide advice and knowledge, but his own researches often formed the centrepiece of my column, being as they were both bold and original.

On the occasion of which I am writing, I had been summoned by a telegram from Lamartine.

"COME AT ONCE. ASTOUNDING DISCOVERY.

LAMARTINE." I showed this to my editor, old Simon,
who audibly sniffed his scepticism, but allowed me
to accept the invitation at the magazine's expense.

"The old boy" (old, indeed! Simon had ten years,
if not more, on Lamartine) "has sometimes come
through with the goods. I want seven hundred
words off you by Tuesday, and this will do as well as
anything, if there's any substance to it whatsoever.
And no cab to the station. You can walk. It will be
good for you." And this, mark you, coming from a
man whose sole notion of exercise was standing up
to light his cigar.

As I mentioned earlier, it was a fine day, and it was
a positive pleasure for me to walk to the station. Little did I know what I would experience before I beheld the streets of Paris once more.

Chapter II

ON arrival at the suburban station serving the village in which Lamartine resided, I decided to walk to Lamartine's house, and on the way there, I purchased a bottle of Armagnac, of a brand to which I knew him to be particularly partial. My visits to Lamartine almost invariably included a meal prepared for me, and I felt it incumbent upon me to return the hospitality in some fashion. Sometimes this took the form of a box of cigars, a bouquet of flowers or box of chocolates for Mme. Lamartine, or on others, such as this, a small bottle of spirits. My gifts were always accepted, with protestations, but it seemed to me to be a poor return for the Professor's generosity of time and spirit.

I was delighted to see Agathe, the Professor's daughter, walking in the garden as I approached the house. In her early twenties, she had inherited her mother's good looks, with fiery hair in which Titian would have gloried, and striking green eyes, rather than her father's slightly eccentric appearance, and it seemed to me that whenever I entered into conversation with her, that she had inherited many qualities of the scientific mind of the Professor, as she almost invariably referred to her father. On several occasions, she had done me the favour of accompanying me to the theatre or to a restaurant, with the approval of her father, and though it would not be accurate to say that we had an understanding, there was something between us that went deeper than simple friendship. I doffed my hat and asked after her health and that of her mother before asking the whereabouts of her father.

"The Professor is round at the back. Shall I take you, or will you make your own way? I warn you, he's very excited about things. No, I can't spoil his fun and tell you what it's all about, because he has yet to inform even his own family of what he has been up to," she smiled after we had exchanged greetings. "I'll let him have the pleasure of telling you himself. But it's great news, he tells us."

Intrigued, I told her that I would find my own way to the Professor, and started around the house to the laboratories at the back. As I made my way, I was nearly knocked over by a small child, pedalling a tricycle as fast as her little legs would make the machine move.

"Hello, Marie," I said, recognising the infant as the child of the Lamartines' housekeeper. "That's a lovely tricycle," I told her, rubbing my bruised shin as I did so.

"The P'ofessor and Mrs P'ofessor gave it to me as a p'esent. Sorry about your leg," she lisped, pulling out a tiny handkerchief and gently rubbing my trouser leg with it.

"Thank you," I replied. "It's much better now. I'm

just going to see the Professor."

"I shall take you there myself," she announced gravely, turning her vehicle as handily as an experienced coachman turns a carriage. She made her slow, dignified way beside me, acting as a kind of guard of honour as I reached the laboratories, which had formerly served the household as stables. "He's in there," she told me gravely, pointing to one of the doors.

"Thank you, Marie," I said to her, and knocked on the door.

"Enter!" came the familiar tones, and I opened the door to discover Lamartine sitting at a desk covered with papers, in their turn covered with his sprawling handwriting. "What kept you, Gauthier?" he demanded, hardly looking up from his work. "I telegraphed you over four hours ago."

I smiled to myself. This was typical of the man, who, while hospitable and considerate in most things, somehow seemed to be unable to grasp the concept that there were matters in the world which were of more importance to others than the affairs of Professor Rémy Lamartine.

"My dear sir," I gently reminded him, "it is not always as easy for me to make the journey to appreciate your discoveries, as it is for you to make the discoveries themselves."

He chuckled. "Very well, then. By the way, I see that you enjoyed little Marie's company on the way here. It is a joy to see her making her rounds, and acting as a guide for the benefit of my visitors."

"May I ask how your researches into the nature of the new gases are progressing?" When I had last visited Lamartine, he was engaged in the pursuit of knowledge regarding some of the rarer elements, such as helium and the recently discovered argon.

"I was hoping that these would combine with other elements to create valuable compounds, but so far, they have resisted my attempts at a forced marriage. No, the reason why I have called you here today is of far more interest and importance than a handful of exotic elements. I determined that you shall be the first to experience this new discovery at first hand. Come with me." He rose, and led the way through a door leading to the next room. "There, what do you make of that?" he declaimed with a flourish.

I gazed at the mechanism before me. Polished brass struts formed a framework supporting a labyrinth of glass tubing connected to shining metal vats, with dials and gauges which no doubt informed the cognoscenti of the status of the liquids or gases contained therein. Polished mahogany rails, at about waist height and supported on more brass rods, stood in the centre of this complex mass of piping, enclosing a horizontal square sheet of thick glass, about a metre on a side, and raised about thirty centimetres from the floor. On the side of the glass platform furthest from us I recognised some electrical apparatus, with Leyden jars and accumulator coils. Copper cables connected these to some of the vats. A white cloth covered a part of the machinery, and more cables led from under the cloth to the electrical part of the assembly. Everything seemed to be of the highest possible quality, as regards both materials and construction, and it was clear that much effort, not to mention considerable expense, had been spent on the construction of this thing, whatever it might be.

"I can make nothing of it," I confessed. "It is hardly one of those constructions where the function is determined by the form."

Lamartine laughed. "I would be amazed if you had been able to work out the purpose of this machinery from its appearance. Allow me to show you how it works." He reached in his pocket and pulled out a watch. "Observe the hour," he said, pointing to the hands of the timepiece.

"A little after three o'clock." I took out my own watch and regarded the face. "I have the same hour."

"Very good," he said. "Perhaps you would do the honours? Please place the watch in its proper location, which is the centre of the glass platform." I took the watch from his hand, and with some trepidation advanced towards the apparatus. "It is perfectly safe at the moment," the Professor called to me. "Simply place the watch, face-uppermost, in the centre of the glass. Excellent," he told me as I did so, and I stepped away. "I will now demonstrate to you the capabilities of this machine." He moved to the cloth-shrouded part of the machinery, and with the showmanship of a stage magician, removed the covering.

Beneath was a mass of controls, reminding me of the engine room of a large steamship. Dials, levers and knobs abounded, the purposes of which were a mystery to me. I expressed my wonderment.

"It may seem to be complex," Lamartine admitted, "but it is actually more simple than it appears. Here, you should wear these." He passed a pair of smoked glass goggles to me, donning a pair himself. "The machine also makes a loud noise when in action, so this may be of use," handing me a wad of cotton-wool. "Use this to block your ears. I trust you are now ready?"

He bent to the controls and made adjustments. A faint buzzing sound started, which grew in pitch and intensity until it became an almost unbearable high-pitched whine, despite the cotton-wool with which I had stuffed my ears.

"On the count of three," said Lamartine, grasping a large brass lever. "One ... Two ... Three ..." He pulled the lever, and there was a blinding flash of light, from which I turned away instinctively. The lightning was accompanied by a thunderous crash. "Look!" cried Lamartine, pointing to the apparatus. There was no trace of the watch on the glass plate. It had vanished from the spot where I had placed it!

Chapter III

"**Y**ou can hardly expect me to be astounded that it has gone," I said, removing the goggles, and pulling the cotton-wool from my ears, "after the noise and thunderstorm you have just created. It is probably in thousands of pieces by now, shivered by the shock of the blast."

Lamartine said nothing to me, but merely smiled.

"And," I added, "I am surprised that the neighbours have not made their feelings known to you if this is the nature of the experiments that you have been conducting." I confess to having been more than a little annoyed by the inconveniences to which I had just been subjected, and despite my respect for Lamartine and his knowledge and abilities, I could not help but show this irritation.

"I confess that their desire to expand the boundaries of knowledge is not as great as my own," he answered me. "However, on this occasion, the effect was considerably more violent than previously, and I anticipate the worst – at least, as regards the non-scientific aspects of the experiment."

As if to confirm his words, there was a knock on the laboratory door, and his daughter entered. "Excuse me, father, but Colonel Legrasse's butler has just called to express Mme. Legrasse's displeasure at the noise of the recent explosion."

"Please pass on my sincere apologies, and explain that I am otherwise engaged, and am therefore unable to express my regret in person. Oh, and," as Agathe turned to go, "ensure that Mme. Legrasse receives a bunch of the finest grapes from the hothouse."

"Very good."

"And the same goes for any other complaints," Lamartine called after her. "You may also add that I do not anticipate any more such disturbances today."

My ears were still ringing from the sudden explosion, and black spots still danced before my eyes. "What was that?" I demanded of Professor Lamartine. "It sounded like a thunderbolt."

"That, my dear fellow, is precisely what it was. A large quantity of electrical force making its way through the atmosphere in the form of a spark, accompanied by the noise which appears to have irritated my neighbours. If it had come from the heavens, they would, I am sure, have raised no objection, but as it is, my production of a perfectly natural phenomenon appears to have caused them some distress."

"And the watch? What has happened to that?"

"That, Gauthier, requires some explanation. I trust that my little lightning bolt has not jarred your mental faculties?"

I shook my head.

"Good. Then let us go to the other room for," here he pulled out another watch from his waistcoat, "another fifty minutes or so. While we are gone, it may be as well to open the windows and release the smell of ozone."

"It is indeed rather strong," I agreed, assisting Lamartine to open the casements. Following this, he covered the controls once more with the cloth and led the way into the room where I had earlier encountered him.

When we were seated facing each other across the desk, he hospitably offered me a cigar, which I accepted with pleasure. "I do apologise to you for the inconvenience. To tell you the truth, I was more than a little startled myself," he added with a smile. "Though there is always something of a discharge on these occasions, today it was somewhat greater than usual."

"And what, precisely, are 'these occasions', if I may ask?"

"You may need your thinking cap here." His eyes twinkled as he took a blank sheet of paper, and a pencil, which he used to place an almost invisible dot in the centre of the paper. "What do we have here?"

"A dot."

"Let us rather refer to it as a Euclidean point. How many dimensions does a point possess?"

"Why, none, I suppose."

"You suppose correctly. Now look." He took up the pencil again and drew a line. "A Euclidean line. How many dimensions?"

"One."

"Imagine yourself to be a creature living in this universe, which consists only of this line. The concept of here," and he placed the pencil point on the paper, some one inch away from the line, "would be incomprehensible to you, would it not?"

I agreed, and he continued, drawing two more
lines, connected to the first line and to each other,
to form a triangle on the paper. "And here we have?"
"Two dimensions," I replied dutifully.

"Indeed so. Our little flatlander can move this way,
and that way. And of course, we know these as the
x and y axes of a graph. But here," and he waved
the pencil above the paper, "is an area that is totally
unknown to our little flatlander. He cannot conceive
of it, any more than we can conceive of the fourth
dimension."

"There are only three dimensions, are there not?"

"You see, my little flatlander, that you are indeed
bounded by what you can perceive. But what I have
been able to discover through the art of mathematics that there is indeed a fourth dimension, and most
probably, though I have yet to confirm it with mathematical certainty, a fifth."

I puzzled over his words and, try as I might, I was
unable to picture in my mind what manner of world
could contain four dimensions, let alone five.

Lamartine observed my puzzlement and smiled.
"We – that is to say – we poor flatlanders trapped in
a world of three dimensions, find it hard, if not impossible, to imagine more. Our mistake comes in im-
agining that these extra dimensions are to be measured with rulers in metres and centimetres. We can,
of course, imagine them to be similar to ours, but
that is more a matter of convenience than an actual
representation, just as this drawing here is a matter
of convenience for our two-dimensional flatlanders."
Here he sketched a perspective rendering of a cube.

I considered his words for a minute. "May I assume
that I would not understand the mathematics that

led you to this conclusion of there being more dimensions than the ones we perceive every day?"

"I think that is a very reasonable assumption indeed. I mean no disrespect to your mental faculties, or to your intellectual abilities, which are undoubtedly superior to those of the average blockhead calling himself a journalist, but I think it is fair for me to say that there are very few people in the world – perhaps only one or two – who would be capable of following my mathematical train of thought. If you wish, however, I will be happy to show you some of my working papers." He smiled, knowing what my answer would be.

"I am sure that these are beautiful, of their kind," I said, smiling in reply, "but their subtlety would be wasted on me. What, though, is the link between these extra dimensions and your thunder-machine in the next room?"

"It is considerably more than a 'thunder-machine'," he exclaimed, somewhat impatiently. "Believe me, if I wished to create a device which was no more than a producer of flashes and bangs, I am sure that I could do better than what is in the next room. No, what I have produced is the practical, tangible fruit of many hours of calculations, and it is nothing more or less than a gateway to the fourth dimension, and possibly to the fifth, and even possibly dimensions beyond that."

"You mean that the watch disappeared into the fourth dimension?" I asked incredulously.

"Yes, in exactly the same way that this pencil point disappears from Flatland when I lift it from the surface of the paper."

"So the watch is now in the fourth dimension?"

"And possibly the fifth and sixth as well," he added, smilingly. "Shall we return to the 'thunder-machine', as you were unkind enough to refer to it?" His tone, as well as his faint smile, persuaded me that he was not seriously annoyed by my describing his brainchild in such terms.

We rose, and made our way into the adjoining room. "Keep your eyes on the glass platform," Lamartine advised me. "If my calculations are correct, and if I adjusted the controls correctly, we should see a result in the next minute at the outside."

Indeed, he had hardly finished speaking before there was a soft "pop" sound, accompanied by a shimmer of light in the centre of the glass plate which lasted for less than a second. When the light had faded, the watch had appeared in the centre of the plate, as I had placed it there an hour earlier.

Chapter IV

"**T**HE famous English magician Maskelyne would be proud of you," I said. "That is as neat a piece of conjuring as I have seen in a while." I spoke light-heartedly, but in this instance Lamartine chose to take my words seriously.

"This is no mere stage illusion," he said, with some heat. "It is the result of my researches into the very nature of the universe. What you have just beheld marks a new chapter in our understanding of the world which we inhabit."

"I apologise for my ill-timed jest," I said. "Believe me, I respect you too well to believe that you would ever resort to such trickery. Perhaps you can explain to me in simple terms what has happened just now?"

"I accept your apology," Lamartine answered, with some magnanimity. "I should have known better than to assume that your words were in earnest. I will do my best to explain what you have just witnessed, without resorting to mathematics, that is to say, as far as this is possible.

"To begin my explanation," he continued, "do you remember that I told you that these new dimensions were not to be measured in metres and centimetres?"

"I do. In what should they be measured, then?"

"In seconds, minutes and hours."

I considered this briefly. "You mean, then, that these new dimensions are time itself?"

"Yes, indeed. They are temporal, rather than spatial dimensions."

"No wonder that I cannot imagine them, since they are invisible to me."

"But you can see their effects, can you not? You are aware of the passage of time and of its effects, surely? And what I have done is to render these dimensions visible, or at least tangible, in such a way that we can move freely along them."

"But how?"

"I can give you an analogy," Lamartine told me. "Let us return to Flatland, and its inhabitants. For our flatlander to travel from one side of his world to the other, he must traverse the width of the paper, must he not?"

"That much seems obvious."

"But what if the paper on which his world exists is folded in half? Then he is able to move directly from one side to the other."

"I begin to grasp your meaning."

"What I have done, I believe, is to bend or fold the fifth dimension so that the relations between the three spatial dimensions and time become flexible. I was able just now to manipulate that watch so that it moved forward in our time, while not moving in space, or its own time."

"What do you mean by 'its own time'?"

"Look at that watch, and tell me what time it

shows."

I moved gingerly towards the glass slab on which the watch reposed.

"There is no need for any anxiety on your part," called out Lamartine. "I am hardly likely to set off the thunder and lightning while you are there."

I was somewhat reassured, and put out my hand to touch the watch. "Why, it is cold," I exclaimed. And indeed it was; condensation, if not ice, was starting to form on the watch's surface, and the glass under it.

"Why, yes. I have observed such a phenomenon previously," answered Lamartine. "I am assuming that all the energy, including much of the heat, has been absorbed by the process. Now have the goodness to examine the time shown on the face."

I did so, and remarked with some surprise that the time appeared to have advanced by only a minute or so since I laid the watch on the glass an hour previously.

"But that is easily explained," I said. "The shock of the lightning and the thunder may well have stopped the mechanism."

"I doubt it very much," Lamartine told me. "Hold the watch to your ear."

I did so, and was amazed to hear it ticking. "Then the shock of its reappearance, however it was accomplished, was sufficient to restart it."

"My dear Gauthier, you must believe me when I say that watches and clocks do not conveniently start and stop in this fashion. I have carried out such a trial with a number of timepieces, including hourglasses, which are not susceptible to shock in the same way, and in every case, the setting of the timepiece is the same on its reappearance as it was when it disappeared. You must believe me on this."

"How many times have you performed this experiment, then?"

"This is my sixth attempt."

"And in every case, the timepiece has returned at the time you expected? That is to say, according to our time, since there seem to be two different times involved."

"Other than some initial slight inaccuracies in the settings of the machinery, which caused some slight discrepancies, that is so. In this last instance, I believe that there was a discrepancy of about thirty seconds in a total time of one hour. That is less than one per cent, and I am certain that this can be made more accurate as my trials progress."

My head was spinning with the implications of this. "I now believe that you have sent an object into the future," I said. "But could you send such an object into the past in the same way?"

"I have successfully done so," he told me. "I have observed an hourglass appear on this glass platform, taken it off the machine, and an hour or so later, sent it back into the past at the time when I saw it appear."

I considered this. "You are telling me that an hourglass that you had never seen before appeared on the plate, you then sent it back into the past, and you never saw it again? And you are sure that it was the same hourglass?"

"That is all perfectly correct."

My head was spinning. "What was the initial source of this hourglass? Had you seen it before? I do not see how it can ever have existed, given that you no longer possess it, and you had never seen it before its miraculous appearance. I fail to understand this puzzle."

"Aha! I knew I had invited the right man to share my discovery," he exclaimed. "You have put your finger on the very point that has been puzzling me also. Where did this object appear from? How was it created, and what existence does it have outside the dimensions that I have discovered?"

"You cannot explain this in terms of the Flatland paper?"

"Try as I will, I find it impossible to fold the paper of Flatland in such a way as to provide an explanation. Only by piercing the paper with the pencil can I come close to an analogy."

I shuddered. "If you are indeed piercing holes in time by sending things into the past, I have many concerns regarding the results of such actions."

"I, too," he confessed. "I have only set the controls to the past that one time, being fearful of any future outcome. However, I am hopeful that this can be overcome as I come to a fuller understanding of the nature of the problem."

"Do you intend to go further into the mathematics to discover the answer?" I asked. "Or to seek help from another?"

"There is no-one in this country who would be able to assist me," he answered. "There are, perhaps, a few in Germany who might understand a little of my methods, but I am unwilling to share my work at this stage. No, there is only one way in which I feel that I can understand it fully. My researches so far seem to indicate that living matter will behave in a different fashion to mere dumb inanimate matter. According to all that I can predict, the vital protoplasm that gives us life, and the spark of consciousness that ignites us, seem to be factors that will influence the way in which the new dimensions operate. Consider for yourself how time seems to pass. Sometimes quickly, sometimes slowly."

A dreadful suspicion came over me. "I think I know what you are proposing. I believe that you wish a human being to take the path that the watches and hourglass have taken before."

"Indeed so. I am prepared to become the first chrononaut in history, sailing into the unknown seas of time."

"It is a risk you should not take alone!" I exclaimed. "If any accident were to befall you in that mysterious dimension, then there would be no help for you."

"Precisely so," he replied, with a sardonic smile. "This is one of the reasons why I invited you here today. When I make my first voyage into the un-known dimensions, I will have a companion by my side. A companion I can trust – that is to say, you, my friend!"

Chapter V

YOU may imagine my astonishment when I heard these words. As a journalist, I had sometimes found myself in strange situations, which at times had placed me in some danger, but never had I expected to encounter anything of this nature.

"Surely," I stammered, "there must be another whom you can trust to accompany you? One of your assistants, for example, with a knowledge of science and your work that are infinitely superior to mine."

"You surely are not afraid?" Lamartine rebuked me.

"I am more than a little concerned about various matters," I told him. "For example, who will operate the controls when we set off on our travels through time? Who will determine where and when we will exit your new dimensions?"

"Why, no-one will operate the controls." He smiled enigmatically, and stroked his short black beard while waiting for my response to his pronouncement.

"So you are proposing that we wander through the unknown world without any control over our destination?"

"By no means. Allow me to explain. An inanimate object, such as the watch that you have just seen, requires its time and place to be set with the control panel. It is unable to make decisions of its own."

"That much is obvious."

"But where does it go when we no longer see it? It is axiomatic, is it not, that matter can neither be created nor destroyed?"

"Very true."

"I believe that it passes into what I call the 'Untime' – that is to say, a state in which neither time nor space have any meaning in the everyday accepted sense. It is a state which is unimaginable to us."

"And yet you have imagined it?"

"I have done more than imagine it, my dear Gauthier. I have proved it mathematically."

I laughed. "I suppose I must take your word for it. You know well that I am unable to follow your steps in your dance through the abstract world of mathematics. But you have proved it, you say? You are certain of this?"

"As certain as I am of any scientific theory," he told me, with great conviction ringing in his voice.

"And you can assure me that there is no danger?"

"I can assure you of no such thing. What I am offering you, as a man and as a journalist, is a unique opportunity to be the first to experience a completely new world. Of course there is danger! What would life be without it?"

"I must consider this," I said. "If I venture into the Apache districts of Paris, or if I fly in a balloon, or attend Army manoeuvres, there is danger. But these are known dangers. I may assess them and provide against them in a way that removes the risk from my actions. But here? You are asking me to place my head in the cage of an animal of unknown temperament. I do not know if I will be embraced or decapitated. Give me time, Professor."

"A day at most," he replied brusquely. "There are others who might not be as cautious, shall I say, as you. There is Daniel from *Le Monde*, for example."

"That scribbler!" I exclaimed. "All he is good for is the reports of the police-courts. Why, the man has all the poetry of a German sausage."

"Or," he continued, ignoring my outburst, "perhaps I might invite Rousseau from *Le Figaro* to accompany me."

"You cannot be serious," I told him. "Rousseau perhaps has imagination, and I confess that he possesses a certain literary style, but he is a raging Socialist. Who knows what kind of complexion he might place on your Untime and his experiences?"

"Who indeed?" replied Lamartine calmly.

"Damn you, Lamartine!" I cried. "You have decided me. I am not prepared to let such rascals as Daniel or Rousseau to introduce your work to the world. I am your man, Professor." He extended his hand to me, and I clasped it warmly.

"I knew I could depend on your friendship," he told me. His smile by now was no longer secretive, but instead betokened a genuine pleasure.

"When do you wish to start?"

"There is no time like the present," he retorted smartly. "We can start at once."

Once again, I was taken aback by the sudden nature of Lamartine's demands.

"At least give me time to prepare my last will and

testament," I said to him.

Lamartine laughed in my face. "By all means, my dear fellow," he answered me. "Though I confess to being somewhat offended by your lack of faith in my calculations, which assure me that such a precaution is completely unnecessary."

"Nonetheless," I retorted in as firm a tone as I was able, "I would welcome the opportunity to set my affairs in order. It is high time that I did so, in any case."

"Very well, since it seems to be of some concern to you. Here is a pen and paper. Shall I call in my daughter to witness the document along with myself?"

This was an eventuality that had not occurred to me, and I had no wish for Agathe to be aware of my lack of faith in her father's abilities. "Maybe, on second thoughts, I will put my trust in your calculations," I told Lamartine.

"Then let us make preparations," he said. "If you do not wish to be frozen on your return, as was the watch, I advise you remove all metal from your person. Your watch, keys, coins, and the like."

"My waistcoat has brass buttons," I told him.

"Off with it, then. The risk of carrying any metal on your person is too great, not only on account of the extreme cold, but of other matters connected with the electric fields."

On searching my pockets for other metallic objects, I came across the half-bottle of Armagnac that I had purchased earlier as a gift for the Professor, and held it out to him.

"Excellent," he said, inspecting the label. "You came well-prepared, I see. Remove the foil covering the cork, and we can then take this with us. Where would we Frenchmen be without this nectar of the gods, eh?"

While he was thus talking, he was divesting himself of his braces, his belt, and his boots, having first emptied his pockets of their contents. When I questioned the boots, he pointed to the hobnails on the soles. My shoes, however, were of the newer, rubber-soled type, and contained no metal as part of their construction.

"Do not expect to be comfortable," he warned me. "I would remove your cravat and collar," taking his own advice as he spoke. "I do not anticipate pain, but we may suffer some discomfort. But we will never know until we experience it, will we?" His eyes sparkled, and there was a joy in his voice like that of a schoolboy who is about to start exploring a forbidden attic rumoured to be full of mysterious treasures.

At length we were both satisfied that we were free of any metallic encumbrances, and in our shirt-sleeves made our way to the other room, where the mysterious apparatus stood, gleaming in the rays of the setting sun.

I remembered Lamartine's earlier words. "You promised that there would be no further explosions tonight, when you talked to your daughter earlier."

"Why, so I did," he replied. "And I intend to keep that promise. You and I are free agents, with our own sources of energy – our bodies – are we not? Unlike the watch, which required a powerful external stimulus to take it into the unknown dimensions, we will travel there largely under our own power, aided by the peculiar conditions provided by my machine."

"So the smoked glasses and cotton-wool are not needed this time?"

"You may wear the glasses if you like – they contain no metal parts – but I am sure they will prove unnecessary. The cotton-wool may well serve to protect our ears from the noise of the gas in the pipes, though."

He darted to the control panel. "Stand on the glass platform. It will certainly bear your weight, Gauthier. There is no call for you to appear so dubious. Ensure that you leave enough room for me to stand beside you." He turned controls and moved levels. "Thirty seconds from now," he said calmly, stepping away from the panel and joining me on the platform.

That half minute was the longest of my life.

Chapter VI

URING the thirty seconds that Lamartine had allotted for the apparatus to become active, I hardly dared breathe, as the noise once again rose to an ear-splitting whine. I noted the exact hour displayed by the clock on the wall. Beside me, Lamartine was coolly counting to himself, "Twenty-eight, twenty-nine, thirty—"

And as he reached the final figure, a dramatic change took place.

I may say, with all due modesty, that I am accounted as one of the better writers for the Paris journals, and I have indeed been praised for my powers of description. However, what I encountered on this occasion would have defeated a Balzac or a Victor Hugo, let alone a mere journalist.

I will try to give you some account of what Lamartine and I experienced, but I fear that it will fall short of the reality.

My first impression was that my body had disappeared, and I was pure mind, such as one some-

times experiences in a dreaming state. Naturally, the
sudden way in which this had occurred caused me
to cry out, but again, as in a dream, my cries were
inaudible.

Also, even though I had the sensation of being incorporeal, I had a strong sensation of choking, and
extreme heat, which caused me to cry out inaudibly
once more. The overall impression was one of terror
and panic, but this did not last for long, and I was
left in a state of calm.

Somehow, though I was still unconscious of my
body, I was aware, as I had never been before, of my
location. Not only my location on the platform, or
in Lamartine's laboratory, or even in France, but in
relation to the whole of the Universe, absurd as it
might seem. Not only that, but all parts of the Universe seemed equally close, or equally distant. A single step (as it were) might take me to the furthest
stars, or to the next room. It was a dizzying prospect,
and it seems to be insanity when I write it in this
way. How, you ask me, could I choose whether to visit
Orion or Orleans? The Milky Way or the Parc Mon-
ceau? The answer is simply that I could make my
choice, with ease. I knew with certainty where I was
and how I could transport myself elsewhere.

And this, mark you, without my being able to see
anything. If I was conscious of anything at all in my
vision, it was of a pale green glow, almost uniform,
and surrounding me on all sides. I could not tell
from where the glow proceeded, or on what it was
shining to produce the slight variations in intensity.

As I mentally explored the whole of the Universe,
sending my mind this way and that, from the Chamber of Deputies in Paris to a planet in a nearby galaxy
inhabited by strange tripod-like creatures resem-

bling three-legged cockroaches more than anything else, I became aware of something else about my surroundings which was, if possible, even stranger than my omnipresence. I was now out of the flow of Time. Time passed me by in the same way that a locomotive passes a passenger waiting on a station platform. The passenger knows full well the nature of a train. He may board it if he chooses. But if he does not choose, he may stand and watch the magnificent machine sweep past him.

Can you conceive of a world without Time? And I begin the word with a capital letter to impress upon you the majestic ineffable nature of the concept. Throughout our lives, we are conscious of the passage of this invisible, intangible force, but we never trap it, or even begin to slow it, and it resists all our efforts to master it. Even in our dreams, we are aware of its presence.

To be free of Time! Can you imagine the sensation? It is almost impossible to describe in words what I felt when I realised that I was Time's master, rather than the other way around. I was suddenly free of the dictator that had oppressed me all my life, and now it was I, Jules Gauthier, who was in control, with an almost god-like power over this most puissant of forces.

Just as I was aware of exactly where I was, I was also aware of when I was. I knew, with the same certainty that told me I could step onto the surface of Pluto, that I could move myself into next week, next year, next century, even. For just an instant, I was tempted to take myself into the land of the Hottentots, at a time two hundred years hence, merely on a whim.

To be master of space and Time! I luxuriated in

the moment. Of course, you will say, since I was experiencing no such thing as Time, there could be no
moment in which I could luxuriate. Very well, then,
I luxuriated.

But what of Lamartine? Where was he? Though
I might be outside the reach of Time, memory still
had its hold over me, and I remembered that I had
arrived in my present state with a companion. As
I had discovered earlier, I was mute, and therefore
shouting for Lamartine would be a waste of time and
energy. Nor, being effectively earless, would it aid me
to listen for sounds of the Professor.

Nonetheless, I adopted a state which might be
termed as "listening", and to my relief, I could discern a faint mumbling which, though the words
were indistinct, still carried something of my companion's mode of speech. I knew it was useless for
me to consider shouting, but I forced my mind to
send out a telegraphic signal, as it were, informing
my companion of my presence.

To my intense relief, I received what could only be
an answer.

"I ... here ..." I perceived.

I continued to send my mental beacon out into
the void, and was rewarded by the sensation of
Lamartine's voice, with its distinctive timbre, sound-
ing clearly in my ear.

"Well?"

"It is ... awe-inspiring," I replied. You must imagine
this conversation as taking place without voices, and
possibly even without words. However, there was no
lack of clarity in our communications.

"Where shall we go? I have a fancy to observe our
legislators in the Chamber of Deputies," he said to
me.

"Very well. At the present time?"

"I think that would be best," he agreed. "For this first journey in the Untime, maybe we would do well to limit ourselves."

Accordingly we stepped (if the action we undertook may be so described) into the Chamber of Deputies in Paris, where we were located at the rear of the chamber behind the seats of the Deputies. The mist that surrounded us thinned, so that we were observing the proceedings through a thin greenish haze. I wished to see more clearly, and prepared to leave the mist, but was interrupted in my intention by Professor Lamartine's thoughts.

"Once you leave the Untime, how will you ever return into it?" he asked me, and the question was a good one. I therefore restrained myself, and observed the Deputies at their work, if so it may be termed.

Some were asleep, some were unobtrusively buried in the perusal of documents that appeared to be closer to sporting journals than papers of state. A few appeared to be alert, and listening to the Deputy at the front, who was facing slightly to our left as he addressed the Chamber.

As we watched and listened, the speaker turned slowly in our direction to face us. A look of horror came over his face, and his words came more slowly, until he eventually ceased to speak, and his face turned pale.

Several of the Deputies (those who appeared to be awake, at any event) turned to follow his slack-mouthed gaze, but even though they were looking directly at us, appeared not to perceive us.

Beside me, I had the sensation of Lamartine chuckling. "Ha! The fools!" he exclaimed. "Let us see." Immediately he had spoken, a small ball of rolled-up paper shot from where I perceived the Professor to be located, and struck one of the Deputies on the forehead. The poor man gave a cry of surprise. Since he could see no-one ahead of him who could have thrown the paper at him, his shock at the assault was perfectly understandable.

Chapter VII

"**D**ID you do that?" I asked Lamartine, scarcely able to believe what had just happened. "Was it you who threw the paper just now?"

"It was indeed," he answered me. The chuckle had not yet left his voice. "And so is this," he added, as another ball of paper seemed to leave our misty envelope and struck another sleeping Deputy behind the ear. This last woke up with a start, and glared furiously around him before standing up and stamping noisily out of the Chamber, shouting loudly that he would have his revenge on those who dared disturb the sanctity of the Chamber.

I could hardly credit my senses. Lamartine, though no longer teaching at the University, was regarded as one of the foremost men of science of the country, and he was behaving like a child, flicking inkblots around the classroom.

"You should not be doing this," I thought to him. "This is unworthy of you and your position in the world of science."

"Why not? It amuses me," he answered me, and a third ball of paper made its way into the midst of our legislators. This time, its destination was not a human being, but an inkwell being used by one of the Deputies, who was writing what appeared to be a very unofficial document on pink notepaper. The ink splashed over the apparent *billet-doux*, and onto the cuff of the indignant Deputy, who turned behind him to discover the source of the missile, only to find all other heads in the Chamber turned in our direction.

I noticed that several of those on our left (that is to say, to the right of the political field) were crossing themselves and muttering, presumably prayers to protect them from the invisible presences that were tormenting them.

"You should stop this," I told Lamartine, as severely as I dared. "These are schoolboy antics."

"Maybe I will cease now," he said, but it appeared to me to be with some reluctance. "You must admit, however, that they are Where shall we turn to next?"

"Perhaps the British House of Lords?" I suggested. "Surely they will have more dignity than our Deputies, with the weight of centuries behind them."

Accordingly, we moved, and were observing the crimson benches of the Mother of Parliaments through the green mist. I say we were observing the benches, as the place was nearly empty. In addition to the Lord Chancellor, who presides over the House, a total of three of the noble lords graced the hall with their presence. One was speaking, but due to his age, and the apparent loss of his teeth, his words were so indistinct that it was impossible for me to distinguish what he was saying, though my abilities in English are generally considered to be above the average.

The other two peers were snoring softly, oblivious to him, and seemingly to everything else around them.

"Have you seen enough?" Lamartine asked me, and there appeared to be a little mockery in his words.

"I have seen enough," I said, more than somewhat disappointed by what I had just seen. "Maybe it is now time to leave the Untime."

" 'Time to leave the Untime,' you say? I hope you are well aware of the irony in your words," he answered. "Very well. We have made two successful excursions into space, have we not? What say you to a little excursion in time?"

I confess that this idea was a little disturbing to me, and I told him so.

"Nonsense, man!" he rebuked me. "As you can perceive for yourself, in the Untime, Time itself is merely another dimension – one which we may bend at will, or even ignore at our leisure, should we so desire."

"Then let us take a short journey only," I said. "Let us return to your laboratory an hour's time from when we started."

"I agree with the time, but let us deposit ourselves outside my front gate," suggested Lamartine. "Are you confident of your ability to do so?"

"As sure as I am of anything in my life."

"Very well, then. On the count of three. One ... two ... three ..."

I took my incorporeal steps in time and space and found myself tumbled on the grass verge outside the gates of Lamartine's house. The sun was considerably lower in the sky than at the time of our "departure" – indeed, it had almost set. I was clad in shirtsleeves, but it was not on account of that, I was sure,

that my teeth were chattering with cold. Professor
Lamartine was beside me, and it was clear that he,
too, was suffering in the same way as was I.

He looked over to me and extended his hand,
which I grasped with some affection and not a little
relief. "My heartiest congratulations, my brave fellow
chrononaut!" he exclaimed. "My God, I am cold! Do
you have the brandy with you still?"

I reached in my pocket and produced the bottle,
withdrawing the cork before handing it to him.

"Here's to Time! Here's to Untime! Here's to you!
Here's to me! Here's to us!" he exclaimed. He took
a long pull at the bottle and sighed deeply. "Many
thanks, my faithful friend." He took another drink
before passing the bottle back to me. I drank in my
turn, and felt the fiery liquid burn its way down my
throat. Now the burden of Time was laid upon me
once more, I felt much as does a swimmer who has
emerged from the water and feels the earth's pull
again.

"Well?" he said, lying on the grassy bank, propped
up on his elbows.

I adopted the same posture, regardless of the sight
we would present to any passers-by; two middle-aged
gentlemen of somewhat full habit, dressed in their
shirtsleeves, and lying by the side of the road.

"It is an amazing sensation, to be sure. Almost
god-like."

"God-like, yes. Indeed, god-like," mused the Professor, his eyes half-closed.

Chapter VIII

WHEN I heard these words, and looked at his face, I feared for my friend's state of mind. An almost idiotic grin of infantile pleasure seemed to possess him, and his hands twitched almost feverishly, as he repeated the phrase "god-like" to himself over and over again. Possibly, I told myself, the Armagnac had proved to be too much for his system, following the extraordinary experience which we had just undergone.

"Come," I said, and helped him to his feet. "We are neither of us decently attired, and I, for my part, am still cold, despite the brandy."

"Very well," he answered. "God-like," he muttered once again, and then to me, "Do you now understand the concept of eternity?"

I considered for a moment. "Is that what we experienced?"

"Can you think of a better term to describe it? Or perhaps you did not perceive it in the same way as did I. What exactly did you experience?"

I told him, as best I could, in somewhat halting language, the sensations I had felt throughout the time I had spent in the mysterious dimensions. As I spoke, Lamartine nodded in confirmation at each point.

When I had finished, he burst out with, "You and I, my dear friend, are the only ones who know of this. Let us keep it so at present. Later the world must know of this – the world *will* know of this," he repeated with some ferocity and a glint in his eyes. "But the time is not yet ripe. I must ask you to say nothing of this to anyone else as yet, and certainly you must refrain from giving any details of any of this in your magazine."

"Old Simon will believe I have come on a wild-goose chase, then," I smiled.

"Oh, pah! I can present you with some discovery or other that will make it worth your editor's while to have sent you here," he said. "An improved diving-apparatus, for example? I recently perfected such a one, which the British Admiralty is currently inspecting. Our own Navy dismissed it as unworthy of their attention, the fools."

"That will do very well. But what do you propose doing about the Untime, as you call it, that we have just experienced?"

"Why, to refine it and to make practical use of it, of course. Do you not see that the man who harnesses these dimensions will have a place in history that will rival the great Alexander, or Julius Caesar, or even our own Napoleon, our mighty Emperor?"

"And you intend to be that man?" I asked. I was now somewhat concerned that the recent exposure to these new dimensions had turned my friend's wits. He had never talked in the past using such a tone, or expressed such ambitions.

"Why should it not be me? You have just seen the fools we and others elect now to govern us. You must surely admit that my intelligence exceeds theirs by a considerable amount."

"I agree, but—"

"The sooner that France is ruled by a man of true intellect, the better the world will be. France will take her place as the mistress of the civilised world, and the man who rules France will perforce rule the world."

His words sent a chill down my spine. Despite all my respect for Lamartine and his scientific ability, I could hardly conceive of him as the supreme leader of the planet. "Come," I said to him, "I will take you to the house, and then I must return to Paris."

"No, no, I will not hear of it," he said. "You must stay to dinner. There will be champagne to celebrate our success."

I was actually happier to hear that I was invited to dinner than to consider leaving the Professor in this state. I was unsure how I was going to explain his mental state to Mme. Lamartine, but I was saved that task when we were informed by the maid that she had retired to bed with a headache. I retrieved my waistcoat and other garments and impedimenta from the laboratory, and made my toilet before meeting the Professor in the dining-room. Agathe was attending her mother, and did not join us.

Dinner, with the promised champagne, proceeded calmly enough. Lamartine seemed to have put his dreams of glory on one side, though I detected something in his eye that was not usually a part of his character and gave me pause for thought.

At the end of the meal we sat with our brandy (the

remains of the same Armagnac that I had brought
with me and which had restored us after our journey
into the Untime) and cigars, and discoursed on general matters. By unspoken consent, it seemed that
we were not to discuss the events of the day. However, when I stood up to take my leave of my host, he
placed his hands on my shoulders and gazed ear-
nestly into my face.

"I will remind you, my friend, that what you have
seen today and what you have experienced is unique.
Only one other in this world has undergone such a
revelation – that is to say, me. I want you to swear, on
your honour as a Frenchman and as a gentleman,
that you will not reveal what has happened today
without my express permission. May I have your
word on this?"

Naturally, in my profession as a journalist, I was
accustomed to keeping secrets. Such a request was
hardly unknown to me. And yet, given the momen-
tous nature of the Professor's discovery, and his extraordinary state of mind, there was something about
this demand that made it unique. The hesitation in
my acquiescence was visible, and a look of anger, almost of rage, swept across my companion's face.

"If you cannot give me your word on this, I will be
forced to take some kind of appropriate action," he
said. The smile which accompanied these words was
no doubt intended to reassure me that they were intended in jest, but the tone of voice in which they
were uttered gave the lie to this.

"Of course I will give you my word," I answered
him. I thereupon swore a solemn oath to him that I
would not reveal his secrets.

"Excellent, excellent," he smiled at me. "You re-
lieve my mind mightily. I will send you the details of

the diving-apparatus tomorrow by post. I think that this will satisfy your editor, will it not?"

"It will, indeed," I assured him, and made my way from his house to the railway station, where I took the slow train back to Paris. The journey gave me ample time to reflect on the events of the day, and on the strange behaviour of my friend the Professor. I had never beheld him in such a secretive mood in the past. Typically, he was only too eager to share his new discoveries with the world, and I could only ascribe the strangeness of his behaviour to the extraordinary events of the day. But his strange and unaccustomed mood was nothing when compared to the turmoil in which I found my own mind. How could I start to describe the feeling of omnipotence that I had sensed while in the Untime discovered by Lamartine? However ineffable the experience, it was one that I found myself anxious to experience once again. The sense of timelessness that I had experienced there was likewise one for which I entertained a fond memory. In the same way that some drugs reportedly take hold of their users, these feelings gave me the strongest desire to repeat them at the earliest possible opportunity. I hasten to add that I had no desire to use these immense powers for my own personal gain or aggrandisement, as it appeared did Lamartine, but the temptation to explore worlds and times which were otherwise unreachable was one which nagged powerfully at my curiosity.

When I at last reached my apartment and took myself to bed, it was a long time before I was able to fall asleep. The words that Lamartine had spoken to me kept going through my head. I could only hope that they were the effects of a temporary delirium caused by the strange journey that we had under-

taken. Although I was in agreement with him that
the government of the day was in need of improve-
ment, I was far from being convinced that Professor
Lamartine was the man who would constitute a suitable replacement.

I could not rid myself of the memories of the time-
less state in which I had found myself, and the immense powers which had been bestowed on those
who entered the Untime. These powers, should they
be exercised inappropriately, would surely cause
havoc of the worst kind. At length, I fell into a deep
sleep from which I woke almost a full twenty-four
hours later.

Chapter IX

I AWOKE, refreshed in body and mind, some twenty hours after I had retired. My sleep had been deep and dreamless, and I was somewhat chagrined to discover that my alarm clock had rung, and I had been unconscious of its call. Obviously I had missed a day at the office of the magazine, but I proposed to inform my editor that I had suffered from a sudden summer chill, which had prevented me from attending to my duties.

On checking my post, I found that Professor Lamartine had been as good as his word, and had dispatched a sheaf of documents related to his diving-apparatus. I determined to produce an article for the magazine, which would explain the advantages of this new invention, and also provide me with the pleasure of castigating our government for their stupidity in ignoring its merits, and allowing the British to take advantage of them.

To create such an article was the work of a few hours only, and I hoped that it would soften the

heart of old Simon when I went into the office the
next day.

When I finished my labours, my stomach reminded me that I had not attended to the inner man for
some time, and I took myself to a restaurant. To my
surprise, I recognised the familiar face of Agathe
Lamartine, who was eating her meal alone at the
next table. At the same time that I saw her, she appeared to notice me, and hailed me with some relief.

"Will you do me the honour of joining me at my
table?" she requested.

"I would be delighted," I replied. I am by nature
somewhat gregarious, and it gives me no joy to eat
my meals in solitary splendour. It was a pleasure for
me to share my meal with this charming young lady.

As I raised my glass in salute, I noted that her usually cheerful face had taken on a serious aspect, and
I felt compelled to ask if anything was amiss.

"Why, yes. The Professor is far from being his usual self, and I confess that I came to Paris – to this
very restaurant – on the off-chance of finding you
here, to discuss the matter. I knew that you lived in
this district, but I do not know the exact address, and
had heard from the Professor that you and he had
sometimes taken meals at this establishment. I confess that I had few expectations of my expedition's
success, and it must appear to be very shameless of
me, I admit, but my little adventure seems to have
borne the fruit I had hoped for."

"Well, you have found me," I smiled. "But please
tell me more of your concerns regarding your father."

"I have never before seen him in such a state," she
told me. "Today he appeared to be a madman, unable to control his emotions. In the space of only
a few minutes he seemed to move from a state of

extreme depression to one of wild elation."

"What were the subjects of his conversation?"

"That is the other extraordinary thing. You know that the Professor has never displayed a keen interest in the political world in the past. But this morning, he read the political news in three newspapers as soon as they were delivered. I have never seen him do such a thing before."

I laughed, though inwardly I was concerned at hearing this news. "Then you need look no further for the cause of his depression," I said. "The news from our politicians is enough to make one laugh and weep by turns."

"There is some truth in what you say," she admitted, "but there is more to it than that. Have you ever heard my father discuss economic theory?"

I shook my head. "No, never."

"And yet this morning he talked of little else other than bimetallism, a topic about which I know little, and have no wish to learn more."

I agreed. "It is strange for him to discuss such matters."

"May I ask what transpired yesterday in the laboratory? When I ask the Professor, he refuses to answer my questions on the matter."

"I fear that I am unable to tell you. My lips are sealed by oath."

A pretty little *moue* came to her face as she heard my words. "I was hoping that you would satisfy my curiosity on the matter. Perhaps you may at the least inform me whether the explosion yesterday that has disturbed his wits?"

"I do not think so." A thought struck me. "You say that the Professor has been like this since the morning. Do you happen to know at what time he arose?"

"For all I know, he never went to bed last night. At any event, when I arose a little before six this morning, he was awake and had obviously been in the laboratory for some time," was the astounding answer. Astounding to me, since I had felt fatigued since our little adventure, and I had just slept soundly and without dreaming for a full twenty hours.

"Then it is no doubt a lack of sleep which has caused these mental aberrations," I said. "Tomorrow will no doubt see him returned to his normal self after he has rested."

"There is more, though," Agathe told me with a note of concern in her voice. "I noticed yesterday that you were greeted by our little pet, Marie."

I smiled at the memory. "Indeed I was, and my shin still remembers it. What of her?"

"Of course, the Professor has acknowledged her existence in the past. Indeed, it is he and my mother who presented her with her tricycle. But today, in the intervals between his almost compulsive new-found interest – one might almost say obsession – with political affairs, I observed him staring fixedly at the little mite, who was on the other side of the garden. If this had happened just once, I would have said that he was in a brown study, and was merely refreshing his mind. However, this occurred on at least five occasions that I noted, and only in connection with little Marie. On at least three of these occasions, he was taking notes, which appeared to be of a mathematical nature. I was unable to see any details."

"I am sure that there is some perfectly natural explanation for all of these things," I said, though I was far from convinced of the truth of my own statement. "Though I cannot give you all the details, I am able to tell you that what took place yesterday was physically demanding, and also was a sore trial to the spirit. Indeed, I myself have only just awakened from a sleep of some twenty hours," I confessed.

This produced a charming little smile, which I confess that I found so attractive that I covered her hand with my own. She did not seem to object to its presence, but suffered my hand to remain there. "You say that you have slept for twenty hours? I take it this is somewhat unusual?" she smiled.

"I have no recollection of its ever having happened previously," I replied. "Eight hours is typically the maximum length of time I spend asleep."

"And yet the Professor would seem to have slept very little, if at all," she mused. "You yourself have not experienced any fascination with previously unremarked subjects?"

"I think not. I can tell you that between my awakening some hours ago and my coming here I have been engaged on the production of an article related to the improved Lamartine diving-apparatus, the details of which he was good enough to send me, and which were delivered to me while I slept."

"Ah, that diving-apparatus," she smiled. "Perhaps that has put him in mind of the politicians, causing his sudden interest in that direction. Did he tell you that those fools at the Hôtel de Brienne had rejected his invention? He is now in communication with the British, much to his disgust."

"Yes, he informed me of that, and I am about to lash and lacerate those responsible in my column, you will be pleased to hear. Maybe you are correct as regards the source of the interest in politics."

"It does not explain differences between my sleeping habits and his, or the interest in the little girl, though."

"Indeed it does not."

"But let us talk of more cheerful things," she suggested, and the conversation passed to the opera, a diversion for which we both shared a passion.

Chapter X

ON my return to my apartment after escorting Agathe Lamartine to the station where she was to catch the train to her home, I pondered the matters we had discussed. I had not, for obvious reasons, informed her of her father's strange words and behaviour immediately following our sojourn in the Untime. It was strange, to my mind, that I had sunk exhausted into a long slumber, while Lamartine had apparently been able to do without sleep. The obsession with politics might well have resulted from the diving-apparatus having been brought to the Professor's attention, but I was more inclined to ascribe another reason, connected with the wild words uttered by Lamartine the previous day.

Then there was the question of little Marie, and the seeming interest taken in her by the Professor. What was the meaning of this? I was unable to come to any conclusion in my mind, try as I might to find a solution.

Before taking my leave of Agathe, I had given her

the address of my apartment, and requested her to contact me by telegram or any means that seemed appropriate, should there be any further developments that he felt should be brought to my attention.

For a few days, I heard nothing. Old Simon took my piece on the diving-apparatus, and to my disgust, pruned it of many of the passages wherein I took the government to task for its stupidity.

"We cannot afford a libel suit, Gauthier," he told me. "And with the government in its current precarious state, such criticism would be unwise."

When, I asked myself, was the government ever in a state other than precarious? But I held my peace on the matter.

However, four days after our meeting at the restaurant, I was awakened in the morning by the delivery of a telegram from Agathe. In it, she positively demanded my attendance at Lamartine's house. I confess to having been slightly reluctant to accept the invitation, but calculated that I could persuade Simon that my visit would result in another article. Accordingly, I wired my acceptance, and set off for the suburbs once more.

This time, there was no welcome outside the house, and when I rang the bell, the door was answered by the housekeeper, who held a handkerchief to her reddened eyes.

"It's the Professor you'll be after, then, sir?" she enquired. "He's not here, you know."

"In fact, it is Mlle. Agathe who is expecting me," I told her, giving her my hat and stick.

"This way, sir," she told me, admitting me to the drawing-room, where Agathe was waiting. She stood and held out her arms to me as I entered the room.

"I am glad you have come, Gauthier," he told me.

"The house is at sixes and sevens. You saw Mathilde, the housekeeper, just now?"

"I noticed that she appeared to be upset. What is the matter?"

"Little Marie has gone missing. The last time that anyone saw anything of her was yesterday afternoon."

"And there is no trace of her?"

"The only sign of her is her tricycle, which was discovered standing by the laboratory."

"And where is the Professor? I was informed just now that he was not here."

Agathe sighed. "The Professor is away. He is visiting a manufactory in Geneva, which is producing parts for one of his inventions. He left yesterday morning, before Marie was discovered to be missing."

"Before he left, how was he?" I asked. "Was he still concerned with politics?"

"No, that enthusiasm faded the next day. I made discreet enquiries of my mother, and discovered that on the evening that we talked in the restaurant, the Professor retired a little after nine o'clock, and arose at half-past seven the next morning, after apparently sleeping soundly throughout the night. The next morning, as far as I was able to tell, he behaved in his usual fashion, and there was nothing untoward in his behaviour for the rest of the day."

I confess I was relieved by this news. "Then we may attribute his earlier eccentricity to a lack of sleep, perhaps?" I suggested. "The news comes as somewhat of a relief to me. I had feared that—" I held my peace, fearing to say more of my fear that the balance of his mind had become disturbed, and she, sensing my embarrassment, forbore from questioning me further.

There was an awkward silence, during which my

companion's attention appeared to be entirely fo-
cussed on a tree outside the window. "I called you
here, because you requested me to call you should
any further events occur," she said at length. "I was
aware that your interest was primarily with the Professor, of course, but it struck me that the disappearance of this little girl fell into the category of the
unusual."

"And so it does," I replied. "I cannot possibly conceive a connection between a missing child and the
Professor's eccentricities, but I thank you for your
invitation, nonetheless. Was Marie much given to
running away and hiding, do you know?"

"By no means. She is always – let us hope and
pray that the present tense is still appropriate here
– a charming and friendly little child. According to
Mathilde, she has never given any trouble or cause
for worry or concern."

"You have searched everywhere, I take it?"

"Everywhere, save the Professor's private study in
the laboratory."

"Why not there?"

"In the first place, because it is the Professor's private study, and secondly, because it is locked, and
there is no way that Marie could have entered it."

I shrugged. "Both would appear to be excellent
reasons for excluding the chamber from your search.
Perhaps I could make a search of my own? It is unlikely that I will find the girl, as I am sure that you
have done all that is possible to find her. However, as
a reporter, I sometimes have to look for small clues
and hints that will help me uncover the truth of a
story."

"As you wish. We will all be grateful for any light
you can shed on the mystery." She led me to the

small room at the top of the house where the child had been accustomed to sleep.

"What is that door?" I asked, pointing to a small door let into the wall opposite the bed.

"It leads to the attics of the house." My hopes that this would prove to be the solution to the mystery were swiftly dashed, however. "It is always kept locked with this padlock here," she added.

I followed several similar false leads as I went through the various rooms in the house. In each case, either the clue had been followed up, and eliminated, or could be eliminated a priori on account of some circumstance such as the one I have just mentioned.

"I will take myself to the laboratories," I announced. "I am familiar enough with them not to require a guide, I think." And so I was, having been escorted through them several times by the Professor and his staff.

I searched the rooms, looking for anything that might provide a clue to the girl's disappearance. I was strongly of the impression, given that the toy had been discovered near them, that the laboratories would hold the key to this mystery. However, there was nothing that provided me with any inkling whatsoever as to her whereabouts.

At length I entered the room where stood the machine that had transported Lamartine and me into the Untime. I confess to experiencing a slight shiver as I beheld the complex mass of pipes and cables that comprised the apparatus, but was unable to determine to my own satisfaction whether I was shivering with fear or with anticipatory excitement.

A quick search revealed nothing of interest as regarded little Marie, but my curiosity regarding the

control panel was piqued. Bear in mind that I had
only witnessed Lamartine operating the controls,
and had not seen the controls themselves in any de-
tail, and also the fact that I suffer from a high degree of curiosity, both by trade and by nature. I lifted
up the white cloth covering the panel, and beheld a
mass of levers, dials and gauges, together with stopcocks and electrical switches.

In the middle of these was a small square of flow-
ered white fabric, which I recognised as the handkerchief with which little Marie had ministered to
my bruised shin.

"My God!" I exclaimed aloud.

"You may well use His name," came a voice from
behind me. I turned. There in the doorway, his face
black as thunder, stood Professor Lamartine!

Chapter XI

"**W**HAT– what are you doing here?" I stammered.

"I think it is I who should be asking that question," the Professor said sternly. He held out his hand. "The handkerchief, if you please."

I gazed stupidly at the little white square of cloth that I held. "I know what it is," I told him.

"I am aware that you know," he replied in a voice as cold as ice. "The handkerchief, if you please," he repeated, and took a step towards me.

It was clear from the set of his face that he would brook no discussion, and I reluctantly handed the scrap of cambric to him. "Where is she?" I asked. "Is she alive?"

"I am certain that she is alive, and unharmed, though somewhat surprised, and almost certainly very cold," he answered me, a faint smile hovering about his lips.

I considered briefly what he might mean by this, but could only come to one conclusion. "You mean that you used that," and I pointed to the Untime apparatus, "to send her forward in time?"

"No, no," he smiled, though the expression was far from cheerful or pleasant. "I have not sent her forward in time at all."

"Then ....?"

"I merely sent her back three years in time."

"But . . ." My mind was a whirl. "What will happen to her? Three years from now – I mean from then – " My head was whirling. "And if she is caught in this trap where she is constantly sent back? But she cannot be, for she would have to be born?"

Lamartine chuckled unpleasantly as I sank onto a convenient chair. "You need have no fear regarding little Marie," he told me. "You know her as Mathilde's child, but Mathilde calls her thus only out of courtesy. Indeed, it is true that Mathilde discovered her outside in the garden, aged about two years old, some three years ago. No-one knew whence she had come, or anything of her background."

"And this is where you sent her?" I asked incredulously. "Back into the garden three years ago?"

"You are absolutely correct, my friend."

"But ..."

"You are going to ask me, are you not, whence she originally came? Who were her parents? You wish to ask me that sort of question?" He shrugged his shoulders and spread out his hands. "I have to tell you that I am unsure. Yes, even the great Professor Lamartine is unsure of the answer," he laughed, but without humour. "Of course, that is not to appear in your magazine, I need hardly add, along with any other matters connected with this incident."

"But this is monstrous!" I declared. "You have snatched away a young child's life, her future, as surely as if you had murdered her!"

"Did she ever have a life?" he retorted. "When was she ever born, we might even ask?"

I pondered this question. "When indeed? But where did she come from if she was never born?"

Lamartine shrugged once more. "I really have no idea. Is it of any importance? She will be well cared for by Mathilde when she is discovered. She will never know of the heartbreaks that come with age, or the pains of growing old. An enviable state, would you not agree?"

I could not understand this callousness that now seemed to have entered into the Professor's soul. Previously, he had been one of the kindest and most sympathetic of men, always ready to help and to share the joys and sorrows of others. This seeming indifference to Marie's fate was a new and disturbing element in his character. There was one further question, which I was burning to ask him, and come what may, I felt that I must know the answer to it.

"What," I asked Lamartine, "of your ambitions to rule the nation that you mentioned to me that evening following our journey together into the Untime? Have you abandoned this wild scheme?"

"On the contrary, my dear Gauthier. Little Marie is a part of my plans. I had to know what would happen when a sentient creature was sent back through the Untime."

I was horrified by his words, which implied an almost inhuman detachment from everyday feelings. "I shall inform the police!" I told him.

His answer to my words was to laugh in my face. "My dear Gauthier, you will not do such a thing, for two reasons. Firstly, the police will laugh at you. If you tell them that I have done away with little Marie, the first thing they will wish to establish is the *corpus delecti*. Without any body or proof of a crime, and without even this handkerchief in your possession," he waved the scrap of embroidered cloth, "there is no such evidence. They will laugh in your face when you tell your story. Or will you tell them that I have sent her back through the Untime? If you do that, I will have the kindness to come and visit you in the asylum where you will be locked away after they have listened to your story."

I considered this. "Very well. And the second reason?"

"The second reason, my friend, is here." He reached in his pocket, and pulled out a heavy revolver, which he pointed at me. "I do not intend to kill you – yet," he said calmly. "I merely show you this to remind you of its existence. And you yourself are well aware of how easy it is to travel through our space and time using the Untime. Should I ever discover that you are interfering with my plans, or informing others of my activities, you know that it is a trivial matter for me to make my way to wherever you may choose to hide, no matter where it may be, and kill you. I hope that this is clear to you?"

I nodded, dumbly. In truth, this new side of the Professor was one which frightened me not a little, and provided me with cause for serious concern.

"You will now return to the house," he continued, in the same calm, even tone, "and report that your search here for Marie has been unsuccessful. Naturally, you have not seen me, or any trace of Marie. I would then suggest that you return back to Paris immediately. In any event, it occurs to me now that I do not know why you are here. Perhaps you would care to enlighten me?"

"Your daughter requested me to come. Her telegram expressed concern at Marie's disappearance."

"Very well. So it was not idle curiosity on your part? Better than I had expected, I suppose. Now go." He gestured with the pistol towards the door, and I took the hint and moved towards the door of the laboratory building, my hand on the handle. "It is unlikely that you will see me again," he added. "Unless, that is, you decide to make my affairs public, or to interfere in any other way with my plans. I do not wish you to visit here again, except in the unlikely event of my extending an invitation to you. I hope I make myself clear?"

"Indeed you do. I will not wish you good luck with your ventures, but I do trust that you will come to a reconsideration of your plans."

"Get out!" he hissed at me through clenched teeth. "You are beginning to irritate me beyond measure, and I will not be responsible for the consequences if you continue in this vein. I will be watching to ensure that you return to Paris immediately. Do not even enter the house. If you have left any of your belongings there, such as a hat or stick, I will ensure that they are sent to you. Remember, I can be with you in an instant, anywhere, should you think of crossing me. Now go!"

I left hurriedly, and, not wishing to invoke Lamartine's wrath, skirted the house, and made my way onto the road leading to the station. I paused to mop my brow and reflect on what I had just experienced. Surely the Professor's wits had been turned by that extraordinary experience in the Untime, and it was my duty to inform the authorities so that he could be restrained and society protected against his wild fancies.

But then I considered that the Professor, even if entertaining such lunacy, still possessed considerable intelligence and persuasive powers, which he would certainly use to assure others that it was he who was completely sane, and convince them that it was I, rather than he, who should be locked away from the rest of the world. No, it would be useless, I concluded, for me to consider such a course of action.

Chapter XII

OR the next few days, I racked my brains, attempting to discover for myself a way in which Professor Lamartine could be brought to a point where reason could be brought to prevail over his mad fancies. There was not the slightest doubt in my mind that he was capable of using the Untime to track my movements and to pursue me with the intention of doing me harm, should I cross him and thwart his intentions.

Nor could I see a way of persuading the authorities that he posed a threat to our society. As he had rightly pointed out, any description of the Untime that I provided to the police would persuade them that it was I, not he, who was suffering from delusions. What, I asked myself, could be the solution?

I sent a message to Agathe, asking her if she had any details of how Marie had come to the Professor's household. She confirmed for me that Marie had originally been discovered by Mathilde some three years previously, as Lamartine had told me,

and had appeared to be about two years old at that
time. Although she had been found well-dressed in
clothes of quality that indicated a certain class, her
true identity remained a mystery.

I had told old Simon that Lamartine was out of
the country, and that in his absence I would attempt to obtain material for my work from Professor
Schneider at the Sorbonne. The savant and I were
acquainted through my reporting of the procedures
of various scientific societies, and it had occurred to
me that Schneider, whom I knew to be no friend of
Lamartine, would provide a suitable ear into which I
could pour my troubles.

Accordingly, I made an appointment to visit Schneider, and at the appointed day and hour, I
knocked on his door.

"Enter," came the stentorian voice of Schneider.
In contrast to the neat, almost fussy, appearance of
Lamartine, Schneider was a big bear of a man, tall
and thick-set, with a mop of wild curly black hair and
a beard that recalled the wilds of Russia rather than
a Parisian salon. "And what can I do for you, Gauthier? The last piece you wrote on our meeting was
not too bad, I must say. Better than the average fare
dished up by your colleagues. Whisky?" Schneider
had acquired a taste for this appalling smoky spirit
during a stay in Cambridge. To humour him, I managed to drink a little of the glass he poured for me
without gagging.

"Professor Schneider," I said to him. "I must ear-
nestly request you to keep secret what I am about to
say, and not to repeat it to anyone, unless I ask you
to do so."

Schneider threw back his head and laughed
loudly. "You, a journalist, telling me I should hold

my peace? Well, this is a change in the natural order of things, I must say! More whisky?" He poured some more of the vile liquid into my glass, and I was obliged to swallow some.

"I am perfectly serious, Professor," I told him. "My life is in danger if this news gets abroad."

"Oho! Is that so?" he asked. "I can see by your face that you are not joking about this matter. I apologise if I treated your words with somewhat less than the respect that they obviously deserve."

"Not only my life, but the future of France, or perhaps even the world, may hang in the balance."

"Serious words indeed, my friend. Tell me more."

I related to him the story of my adventure with Lamartine in the Untime, starting with the watch vanishing in a thunderclap, and then moving to the journey through the Untime undertaken by Lamartine and me, but without details of Lamartine's words or behaviour. I felt it unnecessary to describe the childish behaviour that Lamartine had exhibited during our visit to the Chamber of Deputies. Schneider followed my words with the utmost attention, writing a few notes on a pad of paper from time to time. At the end of my recital, he sat, his large head cupped in his hands, as he digested my words.

At length, he spoke. "Lamartine is correct when he claims that only a few can understand his Untime, as he calls it. Indeed, I have my doubts as to whether he himself possesses a full understanding of it and its potential. Describe to me once again your sensations during and after the experiment where you and he were in the apparatus. You have not yet informed me, though, why you feel your life is in danger."

"I will tell you more of that last anon," I said, and repeated the account of my feelings while in the

Untime.

Again he sat in thought. "Now give me a more detailed description of the apparatus, if you would be
so kind," he demanded.

"I can do better than that," I told him. "I possess a
certain skill in sketching, and I have a trained memory for these things. I can produce a detailed drawing of the apparatus."

"Excellent," he said. "That will be of great value."

I set to work, and in a short time had produced
a drawing which, to my mind, excellently conveyed
the appearance of the mechanism in Lamartine's
laboratory. I used another sheet to reproduce the appearance of the control panel as I had seen it when
I discovered little Marie's handkerchief.

Schneider fairly snatched the paper from my
hands and studied it, making inaudible comments to
himself the while. "What was this?" he asked, pointing to a part of the apparatus.

"A tank for some gas or other. As you probably
know, Lamartine had been investigating the proper-
ties of helium, and it may be that this is the fruit of
those researches."

"Quite possibly," he murmured in an abstracted
tone. "And these are Leyden jars?"

"That is how they appeared to me."

"Very well. I begin to gain some small understanding of the principles involved, thanks to these excellent sketches and your description. I have an idea
that Lamartine's explanation of the events you experienced may be in error, but that is not a matter
that easily submits itself to proof. Now," and here
he turned to face me and looked me directly in the
eye, "you told me just now that your life is in danger.
Why do you say such a thing?"

I related how Lamartine had behaved in the leg-
islature, and the contempt he had shown for the
Deputies. I added how he seemed to have become
obsessed, as I saw it, with the power that the Untime gave to those who entered it, how he had raved
about the government of our country, and how he
saw himself as the natural heir to political power. I
added the threats that Lamartine had made towards
me to ensure my silence on the matter, but ended
my narrative at that day of the Untime, and what I
had been told by his daughter about Lamartine's behaviour on the next day, considering that it was not
yet time to describe to Schneider the disappearance
of little Marie. Schneider heard me out in silence,
gravely stroking his beard. When I paused, he spoke.

"You said yourself that you were fatigued and slept
for an unprecedented length of time, did you not?
Well then, it is obvious that whatever this Untime
may ultimately prove to be, it has a profound effect
on those who enter it. Is it not likely that such an
experience will have widely differing effects on in-
dividuals? Consider the effects of alcohol, for example. Some men may drink a bottle, two bottles,
or even more, and appear in total control of their
faculties. Some will fall down, or even lose consciousness. Some may become maudlin and start
to weep, while others will become pugnacious, and
start a quarrel with the first man they encounter. Is
it not likely, then, that this Untime will have similar
effects on different men, which cannot be predicted
in advance?"

"It is possible," I admitted.

"Have you noticed anything untoward in yourself,
for example? In your own thoughts and actions?"

I considered this for a minute. "I suppose that my

dreams have become more vivid of late."

He looked at me gravely. "I cannot be certain at this stage," he said, "but I consider from all you have told me that the Untime will have an adverse effect on the health of those who experience it. Have you anything more to tell me about Lamartine?"

"Indeed I have," I replied, now convinced that Schneider treated the matter with appropriate seriousness. I proceeded to inform him of my call to Lamartine's house regarding the disappearance of the child, the discovery of the handkerchief in the laboratory, and the subsequent appearance of Lamartine and his threats uttered towards me. Schneider heard all this with an ever-increasing look of horror on his face.

Chapter XIII

"I CANNOT bring myself to believe this," he said at length. "Lamartine has always displayed a streak of – how shall I put it? – instability. But this passes all belief. I am glad you have found the courage to speak out to me. The police must be informed."

I gazed at him, horrified in my turn. "Have you not been attending to my words, Professor Schneider? Lamartine has threatened to attack any who attempt to stop him in his madness. I know from my own experience that his control of the Untime gives him the power to strike at any place and at any time."

"And of course, he would have the perfect alibi," mused Schneider. "He could have dozens of witnesses to provide that he was in Marseilles, for example, just one minute after a crime was committed in Paris."

"Or even at that same time," I added, "if he is prepared to take the risk in going back in time."

"That is one matter that concerns me regarding the

whole of Lamartine's theory. What he claims is contrary to logic and to common sense," said Schneider. "Let us take the little girl, Marie, as an example. You were told that she was discovered by the housekeeper, when she was about two years old, and adopted into the household?"

"That is correct."

"And three years later, when she is aged about five, Lamartine claims to have sent her back to that time. But a number of questions present themselves to me. Firstly, the obvious one, which no doubt has occurred to you. Where did she originate? Children do not spontaneously appear from nowhere at the age of two. We cannot believe that she simply made her appearance into the world in that way, like the demon king in a pantomime."

"It puzzles me also," I confessed.

"Not only that, but we are expected to believe that when discovered, she was three years younger than when she started her journey through the Untime. We should assume, should we not, that she was clothed when Lamartine sent her on her journey?"

"One would sincerely hope that was the case."

"And what were the clothes discovered with the child when she was found by the housekeeper?"

"I was told that she was clothed, yes, and it was mentioned that they were of good quality. I am sure that I would have been informed had they had been ill-fitting. I begin to understand your point."

"And if the clothes were of the appropriate size for the two-year-old child, we somehow have to explain the metamorphosis of inanimate garments miraculously changing their form. It is possible, with some difficulty, to conceive of the notion of the ageing process being reversed in the case of a human body. It is even possible to conceive of a physical object, such as the timepiece that you mentioned, also reversing in time. But for an inanimate object to change its form in that way? No, my friend, we must look for some other explanation."

"You certainly make a good point," I agreed.

"Do you remember what you told me about Lamartine's analogy with the paper and the lines and so on? When he said to you that going back in time using the Untime would be like making a hole in the paper?"

"Of course."

"I believe he was right, though I do not believe that he had achieved a full understanding of the principles at the time he explained them to you. See here." He seized some paper and a pencil and drew rapidly. "What do we have here?" he said to me. "Where is the pencil point?"

"In the centre of the circle that you have just drawn."

"Indeed. And now?" He pushed the pencil through the surface of the paper.

"I do not know. It is no longer on the paper. Perhaps this is Lamartine's fifth dimension."

"Perhaps, and perhaps not." He lifted the edge of the paper, to reveal another sheet underneath. On this paper was drawn a square, within which rested the point of the pencil. "We are now in a different world, are we not?"

I gripped the edge of my chair. Schneider's explanation was even more dizzying that had been that of Lamartine. "I do not know what to say. The prospect is ... terrifying. You are saying that there may be a multiplicity of worlds?"

"Of entire universes," he corrected me. "And in all

probability, not merely a multiplicity, but an infinity of them."

I was rocked to the core of my being by this concept. "It is unbelievable to me that this should be the case," I said. "Why, this would overthrow the foundations of science, were it proven to be true."

"It may be hard for you to believe," said Schneider, "and I do not make the claim that it is the truth. I merely put it forward as one possible explanation of the strange events that you are describing."

"There are others?"

"To be sure. There is, of course, the simple possibility that what you are describing to me is the product of an overheated imagination. No, no," as I started to protest. "I am not saying that this is in any way likely. Your manner and everything that you have described to me so far convince me that this is not the case. I merely put it forward as one explanation that might be advanced by others."

"And you have more explanations other than this fantastical one of the infinite universes?"

"Nothing that suggests itself more readily at present. You are familiar with the work of Henri Poincaré?"

"I am familiar with the name, naturally."

"Maybe you are unaware of his work on clocks and time as they pass through the æther?"

"I have never heard of this."

"Well, perhaps that is not surprising. He has yet to publish the results of his work. I see that there may be some points in common between what I know of his achievements, and those of Lamartine, as you describe them. But my concern is that I do not believe that Lamartine has a full understanding of what he has unleashed, and I fear for the consequences that may result from what I can best describe as his inspired meddling."

"You believe that he may be creating problems to which he does not know the solution?"

"Exactly that. And it is not only he who is ignorant of the solution, I am sure, but the whole of the scientific world is also without a general comprehension of this discovery. Lamartine could unleash horrors and chaos beyond our imagination. I need hardly tell you that it is a terrible mistake to meddle with forces outside your understanding."

"Then he must be stopped."

"Indeed, regardless of any political ambitions that he may possess. In some ways, the political problems are of minor consequence compared to what he may unwittingly provoke."

"I hardly dare to consider the matters to which you refer."

"I am talking about a breach in the very fabric of our Universe itself. That is to say, the forces which hold it together, and which make us believe in the idea of cause preceding effect, and in our ability to make predictions according to scientific laws which we believe to be universal."

"And Lamartine might cause such a breach?"

Schneider threw up his hands. "He might. He might not. It is a risk that the world can scarcely afford to take, would you not agree? You may think I speak wildly here, and you dismiss my words as the result of a personal grudge against Lamartine. It is true that I dislike him as a person, and I have had occasion to find faults in his work in the past. However, I speak as a scientist here, not as a man with human frailties. Believe me, my dear Gauthier, Lamartine is juggling with bottles filled with nitroglycerine. It is not so much a matter of whether he will drop one as when he will drop it."

"So you will help me stop him?"

"Of course! Do you doubt me? We must ensure that his machine is destroyed, and that he is prevented from constructing another such apparatus ever again. I am with you in this absolutely. And, as I said to you earlier, it is essential that the police are informed of this. They can provide us with protection against any attacks that Lamartine may decide to launch against us."

I had not expected such a lively response to my account on the part of Schneider, and I embraced him warmly. "My friend!" I exclaimed. "Together we will save the world!"

Chapter XIV

S UCH sentiments were, of course, easier to express than to put into practice. It was certainly true that if Schneider were to inform the police that he suspected Lamartine of conducting dangerous experiments, there would be a greater chance that he would be believed than if I were to do the same. Nonetheless, Schneider expressed some doubts as to the wisdom of this course.

"In certain circles, it is well known that I have bones to pick with Lamartine. It might appear to be a case of professional jealousy were I to make the complaint."

"And who will believe a journalist?" I asked in my turn.

In the end, we went together to see the Prefect of Police, M. Fournisseur, with whom Schneider had some acquaintance.

My new ally expressed his opinion, without providing details, that Lamartine's current experiments were hazardous, and posed a danger to the area around his house.

Fournisseur spread out his hands in a gesture of helplessness. "My dear Professor," he said to Schneider. "It is not for me to inform the local police in that town how they should run their affairs. They would send me away with a flea in my ear, and rightly so, were I to tell them their business."

"Then I will go further," said Schneider. "I will tell you that the experiments carried out by Lamartine are a powder keg. A powder keg that could place the whole of the country in jeopardy should action not be taken soon."

"Serious words, Professor," said the Prefect. "But they are words alone unless you can furnish me with some more details."

"I myself have witnessed some of the events of which Professor Schneider is speaking," I told him. "While I cannot pretend to anything approaching the erudition and comprehension that he displays, I can truthfully say that I am deeply concerned by the nature of the experiments, as well as by the state of Professor Lamartine's mind."

"Has he caused inconvenience to his neighbours?" asked Fournisseur.

"Why, yes," I answered. "Colonel Legrasse's household nearby made a complaint while I was visiting Professor Lamartine."

"In that case, that may be all that we need."

Professor Schneider, whose face had been turning a deep shade of red while he had been listening to this latest exchange, stood up, and crashed his massive fist down on the table in front of him.

"This is outrageous!" he exclaimed. "I am informing you of a matter that can destroy the whole nation, and you are concerned only with the feelings of

Lamartine's neighbours. This is intolerable!"

"Calm yourself, my dear Professor," replied the Prefect. "You live in a world of mathematical certainties. I, on the other hand, must walk a delicate political tightrope in the performance of my profession. I will send one of my men to visit Lamartine, on the pretext that the neighbours have complained about the noise. They will inspect the apparatus that he is using for these mysterious experiments that you claim are so dangerous, and order its destruction if they determine that to be necessary."

Professor Schneider, who had by this time regained his seat, once again spoke. Although he was seated, his voice still boomed out. "Fournisseur, I will tell you now that from everything that Gauthier here has told me, your average policeman will have no chance of deducing the methods by which Lamartine's apparatus works, let alone discovering its functions. If it makes you happy to do so, then proceed with your plan, but I warn you now that it will be a waste of time."

"Then perhaps you would prefer to accompany my man on his journey?"

I was mentally beseeching Schneider to turn down the offer. If Lamartine knew of his visit, as he was sure to do, not only was Schneider's life in danger, but so was mine. Lamartine was well aware of my association with Schneider, and there would be no doubt in his mind that it was I who was the ultimate cause of Schneider's visit.

"I will go," Schneider said.

"No!" I burst out. "You cannot! It is certain death for you, and for me, if you are to go!"

The Prefect looked at me strangely. "Has Professor Lamartine threatened you in any way?" he asked.

"He has done so, but in no way that I can explain simply. I simply wish to state that I fear for my life."

"This matter is becoming too deep for me, I fear."

"In that case, let me say merely that I feel it is unwise in the extreme for Professor Schneider or myself to come into contact with Professor Lamartine. I wish to state most categorically that I do not want my name, or that of Professor Schneider, in any way associated with this," I said with conviction. "It is most important that secrecy be preserved in this case."

The Prefect looked at me curiously. "I take it you have excellent reasons for saying all of this?"

"Indeed I do, but as I say, they are complex, and at this time I think you would find them to be incredible. I make this request most strongly, and I trust that you will take note of it."

"Very well. Professor?" he addressed Schneider.

"Very well, Gauthier," he said to me. "I would welcome the chance to inspect the apparatus, but I take your point here. Do you, Fournisseur, send your man on his errand, but I fear it will prove a waste of time."

I now saw my chance to play my ace. "M. le Prefect, there is one other matter that I think will be of interest to your man. If he encounters Lamartine, as I am sure he must, he should make enquiries regarding an infant named Marie, who disappeared from the household about a week ago. She is or was the ward of the housekeeper, whom I know only as Mathilde."

The Prefect sat a little more upright in his chair. "Why did you not mention this earlier?" he asked. "This is the kind of matter in which we can offer our assistance, rather than investigating these fantasies that you claim we will not understand."

"I refrained from telling you earlier, Monsieur, for two reasons. Firstly, because the source of the

knowledge of her disappearance might be traced to
me, thereby putting me in some danger. Secondly,
because I know for a fact that you will never solve
the disappearance. There is no body to be discovered, and no trace of any crime at all. But I suggest
most strongly that your man investigates little Marie,
and asks Lamartine if he has any knowledge of her
whereabouts, taking careful note of his reactions to
the questions."

"You say that we will not solve the mystery of her
disappearance. You seem very sure of this."

"I am as sure of your inability to solve this as I am
of the reality of this table in front of me," I answered
him. "This is no reflection on the capabilities of you
or your men, but rather the nature of the disappearance itself."

The Prefect sighed. "I assume that this is all in
connection with this mysterious experiment which
is it beyond our power to understand?" he asked,
with more than a hint of sarcasm in his voice, which
I chose to ignore.

"Precisely so," I said. "If I were to tell you the truth
of what I know, you would order me locked in a lunatic asylum."

The Prefect looked over at Schneider, and raised
his eyebrows.

"M. Gauthier speaks the truth, as far as I am
aware," he said. "There is danger to him, and also to
myself, as he points out. I thank you, Gauthier, for
your stance in this matter. It is not for myself, but
for Gauthier's sake, that I now withdraw my offer to
accompany your officer."

"Very well, then," the Prefect replied. "This is one
of the most extraordinary meetings of my life. You
are telling me about crimes that it will be beyond my

power to solve, and that you fear revenge from the perpetrators. I suppose that you will be demanding a police guard about your persons next?" He spoke mockingly, but I decided to take him at his word.

"That would be most welcome, M. le Prefect," I told him.

Fournisseur blinked in surprise. "I was not expecting that answer, as you may guess, but having made the offer, even if it was made partly in jest, I suppose I must honour it. Provide me with the details, and I will make the arrangements for you."

Chapter XV

WE left the Prefecture, having arranged with Fournisseur that suitable police guards would be provided for both Schneider and me. It was galling not to be able to provide fuller details of the danger that we were in, but Schneider and I agreed that the truth as we understood it would be regarded as ridiculous by the authorities.

We had been informed that it would be a few days before the police guards would be made available to us, a circumstance that caused me a little concern. In that time while we were waiting for the official wheels to turn, however, a singular series of events occurred.

Old Simon, my editor, came to my desk at the office the day after Schneider and I had visited the Prefect.

"There has been a strange event reported near Vincennes," he informed me. "It would appear that a strange mechanism, which appears to be the apparatus for some sort of scientific experiment, has been discovered in an abandoned house in that area. Some builders who were making repairs to the property came across it. One of them was obviously hoping to make some money from the news and contacted a friend of mine who works for a daily newspaper, who in his turn passed it on to me. Perhaps you can make some sort of story out of it. Go and investigate, and if it seems interesting, maybe we can afford to send a photographer later."

And with that, I was sent on my way, having been provided with the address of the house, as well as of the firm of builders who claimed to have made the discovery. I decided to visit the house first, given that the mysterious machinery had been discovered there. On presentation of my card to one of the workmen, I was introduced to the foreman of the gang which had discovered this mysterious device, a villainous-looking rogue who gave his name solely as "Gérard", and who let me into the building. As I had been told, the house was abandoned, and everything was covered with dust.

"It's in here," said Gérard, opening a door and holding out his hand, obviously in expectation of a *pourboire*.

I gratified his cupidity, and entered the room alone. Gérard hovered by the doorway, watching my actions curiously. The daylight was filtered by the grimy shuttered windows, and it was difficult to distinguish the shapes inside the room, but as I examined them closer, my astonishment knew no bounds. It swiftly came to me that I was looking at a duplicate of the apparatus I had seen in Lamartine's laboratory. If my memory served me correctly, there were one or two minor differences between the apparatus in front of me, and that which I had seen earlier. As with the mechanism in Lamartine's house, the control panel was covered by a cloth. When I moved to examine the apparatus more closely, though, it was clear to me that it had not been used for some time, maybe even for a number of years, as the dust on it lay thick, and seemingly undisturbed. The square glass plate, similar to the one on which Lamartine and I had stood for our trip to the Untime, was opaque with dirt.

In a flash, it came to me what I had to do. "No-one is to enter this room until I return," I told Gérard, who regarded me with an air of amused perplexity. I dashed out into the street and hailed a passing cab to convey me to the Sorbonne, where I dismissed the driver, and fairly ran along the halls until I reached Professor Schneider's office, only to be informed that he was delivering a lecture.

"Where? Where?" I cried, and upon receiving directions, took myself at full tilt along the quiet corridors of the University to the lecture theatre, which I entered without ceremony. The students to whom Schneider was expounding his theories must have been taken aback by the sudden appearance of a wild-eyed man with his garments in a state of disarray, waving his stick, and demanding in a loud voice that their professor should accompany him immediately to an unknown destination.

To his great credit, Schneider patiently heard me out, and acquiesced immediately to my demands, dismissing his class.

"Now then, Gauthier, is there something amiss?" he said, in the tones of one humouring a dangerous lunatic.

"Nothing amiss, but it is essential that you come to Vincennes this instant," I told him. "There is the

most extraordinary thing there that demands your
attention. Do not bother yourself with a hat or over-
coat, but come now."

Still giving me the impression that he considered
me out of my senses, Schneider followed me to
the street, where I hailed another cab to take us to
Vincennes.

"Will you not tell me something of what all this is
about?" Schneider asked me.

"All in good time," I answered him, forcing myself to remain outwardly calm, though my mind
was churning through the possibilities connected
with my discovery. Schneider visibly chafed at my
reticence, but refrained from asking me further
questions.

At length we reached the house in Vincennes, and
Gérard regarded Schneider and me with a sceptical
eye.

"I wasn't sure that you would be coming back," he
said in a surly tone. "And if he's going to go in there,"
jerking a thumb at Professor Schneider, "it's going
to cost you extra."

"Very well," I said, and dropped another few francs
into the outstretched palm.

"Now, what do you make of this?" I asked Schneider,
when we had entered the chamber.

"No-one has used this room for years, by the look
of it," he answered, coughing as the dust caught
his throat. "But what is this?" he asked, on catching
sight of the apparatus. He gazed at it in silence for
a few minutes, and then spoke. "This bears an un-
canny resemblance to your drawing of Lamartine's
contraption, does it not?"

"It is almost identical to the one I saw in his laboratory," I responded.

"But... but... he told you that it was a new discovery, and that he had only just perfected it, did he not?"

"That is so."

"And yet it is clear that this has not been seen or touched for at least a year. You agree?"

"Indubitably."

"Come, let us shed some light on this." He moved to the casement and flung open the shutters, allowing us to examine the mass of pipes and wires. "This is most interesting," he murmured to himself, as he moved between the Leyden jars and the electrical cables connecting them to the control panel. "Most interesting," he repeated, examining the vats and piping. It was a fascinating experience to watch the Professor at work. He appeared to be soaking up knowledge and understanding as readily as a sponge absorbs water. For a short period, his brow would furrow, and his face contort as he came to a fresh part of the mechanism. He would then use his large, but surprisingly skilful, fingers to turn, prod, tweak and otherwise manipulate the subject of his investigation. Suddenly he would release his breath in a long drawn-out sigh of satisfaction, and his expression would clear as an understanding of the apparatus came to him.

"Let us see, now," he would say to himself, pausing at one of the valves set into the mass of tubing. On turning the valve, a small amount of liquid might dribble into the palm of his hand, which he would then examine closely, perhaps sniffing at it, or even, on one occasion, tasting it. "Do not worry, Gauthier," he called to me on one of these occasions, as he caught sight of my astonished face. "There really is little or no danger attached to this."

At length he moved to the control panel and removed the cloth cover before using it to wipe the dust gently from the surface of the panel. He stood in silence examining the machinery before him for at least five minutes, and then called to me.

"Gauthier, you have your notebook and a pencil with you, I take it?"

"Naturally."

"Be so good as to draw these controls, taking careful note of the setting of each one."

I set to work, and though I did not understand the workings of the levers or the meaning of the dials and gauges that I was drawing, managed to produce a sketch which captured the control panel as we had found it.

"Can you tell me what has happened here?" I asked Schneider when I had finished. "What is the meaning of this apparatus? Who built it, and when?"

"Do you need to ask who built it?" Schneider asked me. "Obviously this is Lamartine's work. As to when it was built, I would say that it will be built very shortly, approximately six years ago."

Chapter XVI

SCHNEIDER'S words astonished me. "Your words make no sense. How can you use the future to describe an action that has happened in the past?" I asked. "What we have here stands before us already completed, and seemingly untouched for at least a year or more."

The Professor said nothing in reply, but merely smiled in a way that I found to be irritating in the extreme. I stood there, attempting to reconcile his words with the evidence before my eyes.

"I have it, I think!" I exclaimed, as light dawned in my mind. "You mean that at some point in the near future, Lamartine will use the machine at his laboratory to travel in the Untime to a few years before the present, will do whatever he has to do at that time, and, armed with the knowledge that he currently possesses, will construct this apparatus to return him to the time from which he originated!"

"Yes, that is what I believe," Schneider said to me. "Either he will depart our time in the near future, or it is conceivable that he has already done so."

"And do you believe he will return soon?" I asked.

"I think that it is most probable that Lamartine will return to a time very close to when he enters the Untime, so as not to alarm any by his absence from this world." Schneider had returned to an examination of the apparatus. "To whom does this house belong? Do you know? Does the workman who admitted us?"

"I can ask," I replied, but it seemed that Gérard had no more idea than we, having been employed simply as the foreman of a gang of workmen who had been employed to put right a house in a poor state of repair.

"Listen, my man," said Schneider, who had interrupted his study of the apparatus and joined the labourer and me outside the room. "When is this work due to be finished?"

"Two weeks from today," said the other.

"How much will it take for it to be three weeks?" Schneider asked him.

"I don't understand what you mean."

"I require the undisturbed use of this house for one week, starting from today. That means that you and your men will stay away from this house for one week. How much money do you require for this to happen?"

I was astounded by this extraordinary request, but Gérard seemed to take it in his stride. "Well, there's three of us as well as myself, and we'd want our wages for that time, monsieur," (I noticed that his speech had become slightly more deferential given the possibility of more money coming his way) "and then there's got to be something else on top of that for the trouble. Someone's got to explain it to the boss, after all."

"How much?" asked Schneider.

Gérard named a sum which I personally considered to be outrageous, but it appeared to satisfy Schneider.

"When do you want us to leave?" asked the workman.

"Immediately," answered the Professor, and withdrew his purse from his pocket before counting out the specified sum into Gérard's hand. "Now go, all of you, and I warn you that I do not want to see any of you again before this time next week. You may leave your tools here. It may be that we will require them. The sum I have given you is easily enough to cover the cost of any damage that we may cause to them, and I am in no mood for further bargaining." He glared ferociously at the smaller man as he said these words.

"I understand, monsieur," replied the workman, and took his leave of us.

"What do you mean by this?" I asked, when the sounds from below had ceased, informing us that the workmen had departed.

"I believe, that thanks to your having located this apparatus, I can discover the principles by which Lamartine has achieved his results. It is clear that some of these tanks and vats will need to be refilled with the gases and liquids that they originally contained, but that is merely a matter of a day or so, with the assistance of the University laboratories."

"And then?" I asked.

"And then, my dear Gauthier, I intend to take myself into the Untime, as did you and Lamartine."

I was appalled at his words. "You cannot, should not, do this," I told him. "You said yourself that a journey into the Untime could cause some sort of damage. Are you prepared to risk your life, your sanity, your intelligence, your very mind, simply to satisfy your curiosity?"

"Indeed I am," he said to me. "I believe my intellect to be strong enough to survive the Untime, whatever it may have done to Lamartine."

"I still consider it to be a foolhardy and unnecessary risk," I said to him. "After all, Lamartine designed the machine and was familiar with its workings and with its principles of operation. With the greatest respect, Professor Schneider, and I mean no insult here, you are approaching this matter from a position of relative ignorance – relative, that is, to a man who has presumably spent many years of study investigating the matter," I added hurriedly, as I saw Schneider's face change at my words.

However, Schneider stood his ground. "I have several advantages over Lamartine. Firstly, I have the benefit of your account, and your experience. I know with certainty that this machine is capable of doing what it is intended to do, which is considerably more than Lamartine did when he commenced its construction. Secondly, I have the benefit of a greater knowledge of the work of Poincaré on the subject. Lamartine quarrelled violently with him some years back – indeed, there was talk of their fighting a duel – and I am sure that there has been no communication between them since then. Lastly, I consider my intellect to be stronger, and my constitution more resilient, than that of Lamartine, or even of you, intelligent and healthy as you may be. I have faith that I will survive the experience, and return from this Untime in full health, wiser and with more knowledge than when I started. Now, may I count on your assistance?"

I was not fully persuaded by Schneider's air of confidence, but I had to admit to myself that his words made a certain kind of sense. "I am reasonably certain that I can persuade my editor to allow me the time to assist you."

"Very well," said he. "Let us clean the apparatus first. This will help us to determine what we need in order to put it into full working order."

We stripped off our coats and rolled up our sleeves, but it was soon obvious that we would need more in the way of cleaning materials than the few rags we discovered in the room. However, following an extensive search of the house, we discovered a cupboard stocked with the cloths and polishes that Schneider deemed necessary to place the apparatus in a state where it could be examined and operated.

"I had never imagined myself as a charwoman," I said to Schneider after the first thirty minutes of hard work. My hands were black, and so was my face, if the state of Schneider's countenance was any guide. However, the apparatus was starting to appear much cleaner than before, and it was possible for me to recognise the brass and other materials that had composed the machinery at Lamartine's laboratory. We worked solidly for another two hours or so before Schneider called a halt to our labours.

"Excellent," he said, and wiped his already dirty forehead with a greasy hand, thereby depositing more grime on his face. "We have made excellent progress, but I fear we will not be welcome at the better dining establishments. I suggest that we visit a Turkish bath in order to repair the damage done to our appearances, and resume our tasks tomorrow, which would be better performed in more appropriate apparel."

"Very well," I said. "That sounds like an excellent
plan."

Following our sojourn in the bath, I took my leave
of Schneider. Although he seemed to be interested
purely in the scientific and technical aspects of the
machinery that we had discovered, I had another
object in view; one which was not in the scientific
realm, but which nonetheless promised to supply
some answers to the mystery of the machinery in the
deserted house.

My card identifying me as a writer for my magazine
opened doors in the neighbourhood of Vincennes
that would otherwise have remained closed to me,
and I was able to obtain the information I sought. It
came as little surprise to me, although it confounded
common-sense.

Chapter XVII

I REALISED that some risk, both to me and to Agathe, was incurred by my communicating with her, but it seemed to me to be imperative that I verified the truth of the answer to my question, which I already suspected. Accordingly, I dispatched a telegram to her, signed only with my initials, and inviting her to meet me at "the usual place", by which I meant the restaurant where we had met previously, and the meaning of which I hoped she would understand. Though I knew that these precautions would not deceive her father for longer than a minute, I had hopes that they would at least prevent any servants from informing him of the meaning of my message, should they chance to see it, and be subsequently questioned by him.

At the appointed time I was waiting at the restaurant, and to my intense relief I espied Agathe making her way through the crowd towards me. I stood up and greeted her warmly.

"Does anyone know you are here?" were my first

words.

"How mysterious you make it all sound," she smiled at me. "No, no-one knows. I simply told the servants I was going out for the evening, but did not mention my destination or my companion."

"And I trust that you have the telegram with you?"

"Why no. Is there a reason why I should have brought it."

I sighed inwardly. "No, there is no reason," I told her, trusting that she would be unaware of my disquiet and concern that Lamartine might discover it and follow her trail.

"Why have you invited me here?" she asked me.

"Of course, I enjoy your company, and if I may be so bold as to say so, I enjoy gazing into your beautiful eyes," I said, as light-heartedly as I could manage. She smiled in reply. "However, there is another reason. Perhaps you can tell me something about your father. I know little of him other than what he has told me, and almost nothing of his life before I met him just over one year ago. Where was he, for example, six years ago?"

She furrowed her brow prettily as she searched for the answer. "Six years ago, I remember that he went to Brazil, and then to Argentina. He was offered some sort of place at some of the universities there. He stayed there for several years. A little over three years, as I recall."

"And tell me, Agathe." I leaned forward in my excitement. "Tell me, was he absent from your house when little Marie was found? When Mathilde came across her?"

My pretty companion smiled. "You seem to have an obsession with little Marie and her discovery. She is still missing, though," and her face turned serious.

"It is most mysterious. I have no idea where she has gone, and the police are baffled. In answer to your question, yes, he was away at that time."

"The police are now involved?"

"Yes, an agent called the other day to say that there had been some complaints regarding the explosions in the Professor's laboratory. While he was talking to me, Mathilde burst in and proceeded to tell him about Marie's disappearance."

"What was your father's reaction to this?"

"He is still away from the house."

"And the police are investigating?"

"It is strange," she mused. "When the agent was informed of Marie's disappearance, he did not seem as surprised or concerned about it as I might have expected, given the circumstances. But yes, he dispatched a few more agents who made a search, but they found nothing, and we have been assured that the local gendarmerie is now aware and will be looking out for her."

"That is all to the good, I suppose. But let us return to the Professor. He was away in South America for all that time, you say?"

"That is correct."

"And did you or your mother ever go out to visit him during that time?"

She shook her head. "No. The Professor told is that the conditions there were too dangerous for us to visit, especially for a girl of my age, and even though I begged him to let me visit, he continued to send refusals in his letters."

I was now confident that I had most pieces of the puzzle, and I quizzed Agathe some more regarding her father's state of mind on the occasions when she had last seen him a few days earlier.

"As I told you before, he appeared to be obsessed with politics on the day after you visited and there was a loud explosion, but the next day he said nothing about it. He did seem to be distracted by little Marie, though." She paused in thought and then looked at me strangely. "I believe that you know what has happened to her. It is something terrible, is it not? Can you tell me?"

"I will tell you everything, my darling." The endearment fell naturally from my lips, and though it was the first time I had ever addressed her in this way, it seemed to be natural for me to do so. To my astonishment, she smiled back at me, with a look of what appeared to be encouragement at my words. This gave me the confidence to go on with what I felt I must tell her. "Agathe, it is your father who has stolen Marie," I said to her.

A look of disbelief, mingled with horror, stole over her face, as the import of these words crept over her. "But why would he ever do such a thing?" she asked.

"It is all in the name of science," I said to her. "Your father is undoubtedly one of the scientific geniuses of the age, but in this instance, he is involved in an affair holding great danger for anyone connected with it." As briefly and as simply as I could, I described to her the disappearance of the watch that had caused the thunderclap, and the principles that the Professor had explained to me. It was clear that Agathe Lamartine was a true daughter of her father. She followed my words and my explanation, at times interjecting some comment or question that showed that she was in full understanding of my words.

"There is more," I told her, and proceeded to give her an account of the journey that her father and I had undertaken together to the Untime. As best I could, I described the almost ineffable nature of the Untime, and the feeling of power that I experienced over Time and space. As I described her father's words and behaviour during our sojourn in the Untime when we visited the Chamber of Deputies, and also on our return from that mysterious dimension, I could see her face cloud over with dismay.

"I cannot believe that Father would act and speak in such a way," she exclaimed. The fact that she referred to him as "Father", rather than her usual appellation of "the Professor" indicated to me the depth of emotion to which my words stirred her.

"Believe me, Agathe, this is true," I assured her. "Remember his strange obsession with politics the next day, and his changed behaviour."

"Indeed so. You think that this Untime was the cause of the change in his character?"

"I am sure of it," I told her.

"But what has all of this to do with Marie?" she asked. "Surely he would not treat that darling little infant as he did a watch? O tell me that this is not so, please."

"I cannot do that," I said, simply, and she gazed at me in horror.

"Then where— when— what has happened to the child?" she cried, in such a tone that the diners at other tables turned to look at us.

"Please, my dear, be quiet," I begged her, once again seizing her hand in mine, an action which did not seem to displease her. I told her of my discovery of her father in the laboratory on the day when I had visited to help search for the missing child. When I came to the part of my narrative where I described her father threatening me with a revolver, she drew in her breath sharply and put released her hand from mine, before putting both hands to her cheeks.

"It is an incredible tale that you are telling me, Jules," she said to me, using my Christian name for the first time in my memory, as I continued with my tale. "But I do not believe that you are inventing this story."

"There is still more that I must tell you," I said to her. "I have been making enquiries. During the time that you believed that your father was in South America, your father wrote to you regularly?"

"Oh yes, indeed he did. But why do you say 'believed'?" she asked, curiously. "He had a strange arrangement, though. All the letters he sent to us passed through his university department, where he still held a position, and came to us in envelopes with French stamps, posted from Paris."

"Really?" I said. "That must have been a sad disappointment."

"It was, indeed," she said. "And I was surprised how little about Brazil and Argentina he had to tell us in his letters. I was looking forward to reading about those places, but the letters were chiefly trivial enquiries about our health and so on."

"And when you replied, where did you address the letters?"

"To the university department, and they would forward them to him in America."

"Agathe," I said to her, placing my hands on the table, and leaning forward, "Several trustworthy persons have sworn to me that they saw him in Paris during the time that you believed him to be out of the country."

Chapter XVIII

SHE shrank back, as suddenly as if I had made a move to strike her, and then sat silently in thought for a few seconds. "These people who swore to you that they had seen him, what manner of people were they?"

"Of the lower classes," I told her. "One old woman who told me that she had been your father's housekeeper in a house in Vincennes. The details she provided were most circumstantial. There was also an old coal-heaver who described a man who could only be your father who lived there for a few years."

"I suppose I must believe you are sincere when you tell me all of these things," she said. "But it seems so hard to believe such a thing about one's own father."

"I can only give you the facts as I see them," I replied. "They may admit of another interpretation, but I find it hard to construct any other."

"And Marie?" she asked.

"I told you just now, did I not, of your father's words to me."

"Poor little Marie." She sat in silent thought for a while, and burst out with, "If I understand what you are saying, we will never see little Marie again."

"I am afraid you are correct, as far as I can tell," I told her gravely.

"But what can we do? Poor Father, I fear for his sanity and his happiness."

As it happened, this was a long way from being my major concern, but I held my peace on the matter. "I have enlisted the assistance of Professor Schneider," I said to her.

"That great hulking bear of a man!" she exclaimed indignantly. "Why, if you only knew how he hates my father!"

"I believe he is sufficiently in control of his emotions for that not to play a major part in influencing his actions. He has confessed the enmity between himself and your father to me, but he makes no attempt to dissemble, or to conceal this. I sincerely believe that he is guided by other motives in his wish to stop your father." I told her some more of Schneider's fears that the Untime might lead to the destruction of our Universe as we currently understand it, and told her of the machinery we had discovered in the abandoned house in Vincennes.

"Do you have an explanation for this?" she said.

"Indeed I do. I believe that your father has already gone back to that house in Vincennes a few years before this. I have been to see the letting agents today, and I discovered that a man, very much resembling your father in appearance, was the last tenant of that house. The lease expired only recently, even though there has been no-one living there for some time. In the past, he will use the knowledge he now possesses to build himself a machine that will return him to the future – his future, that is. This time in which we live now, or rather, a short time from now."

"And all this business has occurred, or will occur – I hardly know how I should express this – while he was supposedly in South America?"

"I believe so. By going into the past, one raises the question of the possibility that one is in two places at one time. This, of course, could lead to paradoxical situations where one might easily meet oneself. Imagine meeting yourself, and causing an injury to yourself. Would oneself, the later version of oneself, that is, feel the effects of that injury?" I laughed lightly, but she considered the matter with all seriousness.

"Or," she ruminated, "perhaps if one travels into the past, the person that one was at that time, that is to say the earlier self, disappears from that time? In that way, it would be impossible to meet oneself, or..." She considered her own words for a short while. "But that cannot be, can it? "

"I do not know. I can ask Professor Schneider when I see him tomorrow. Indeed, I wish that you would come tomorrow and meet him, and see for yourself what we have discovered in the house at Vincennes."

"I am beginning to understand what you are saying. While my father was in the past – the past relative to our time now, I mean – it was impossible for him to also exist at the time to which he was travelling from now. It was therefore necessary for him to disappear from view, as far as we were concerned, at the least, and the easiest way for him to do that was to pretend to take an extended trip abroad."

My head was spinning with the complexity of the ideas that were passing between us. "It is perfectly possible that you are correct there. You must certainly meet Professor Schneider and tell him what you know, and also what you feel may be the truth. I told you truthfully that he has no love for your father, but I do believe that he has a respect for his theories and for his discoveries. He would listen to his daughter – you – and your suggestions and ideas with more respect than he would give to mine, I am sure."

"Then I will visit you tomorrow. The address?"

I gave her the address of the house, but warned her, "I do not think it would be wise to write this down. Should your father somehow return and come across it, he will no doubt recognise it, and ask you for its meaning. Rather, you should commit it to memory." I asked her to repeat the address until I was confident that she had it by heart. "And you will come?" I asked. I fear that my voice betrayed my anxiety, for she turned and bestowed on me a sweet smile.

"You should have no concern regarding that. You have persuaded me that there is cause for concern, and yet..." Her voice tailed off.

"What is it, Agathe?" I asked anxiously.

"It is nothing really. This whole affair seems too incredible – almost impossible – for me to consider seriously. Are you quite sure that your experience in this machine has not turned your own wits?"

I laughed. "I have the evidence of the letting agents as well as that of those whom I have questioned," I pointed out to her. "There is also the evidence of the machinery in the abandoned house, which is identical to that I have seen in your father's laboratory. This is not simply a fancy in my head, believe me, Agathe."

"Poor father!" she said, sighing in a manner which I found to be most fetching. "I knew that he was under some strain, but I had no idea that he was suffering in this way."

It was touching to observe the degree of filial devotion the Professor aroused in his daughter, but I could hardly be expected to display sympathy for a man who had threatened me with a loaded revolver and promised to hunt me down should I fail to obey his commands.

"In any event," I said, "he is not showing himself at your house, even if he is, as I believe, concealing himself in his laboratories?"

"That is correct. He informed us a few days ago that he would be away from the house on business. Of course, you may well be correct, and he is living in the laboratory at present."

"Then, Agathe, I must ask you to help us before you pay your visit tomorrow. I wish you to return to the house and search his study for any papers or anything that might appear to have any relevance to this business of the Untime, and then bring those papers to me?"

She bit her lip as she turned these words over in her mind. "His study is usually locked," she told me, "but if you really consider it necessary, I could probably find a way to enter it. However, from what you say, most of his notes will be in his laboratory, and if you feel that he is there, and in no mood to deal with others, it would be foolish in the extreme for me to attempt to enter."

"I would not dream of placing you in danger," I assured her. "I simply ask you to do what you can."

"I have only known you a short time, Jules," (again my Christian name!) "but I know you to be an honest and level-headed man. You know that I am devoted to my father, but as a result of what you have just told me, I will help you, and through you, will aid him!"

In a fever of admiration and of affection – nay, love! – for this remarkable woman, I snatched up her hand and pressed it to my lips, covering it with ardent kisses. She smiled at me, and suffered her hand to remain in mine a little longer before withdrawing it. At that moment, despite the danger that we faced, I believe I was the happiest man on this earth.

Chapter XIX

THE next day saw me at the Vincennes house, once more engaged in the cleaning of the apparatus that promised to lead us to the Untime. I had attired myself somewhat more appropriately for the occasion, and I no longer cursed so frequently as the dirt and dust from the machine transferred itself to my garments.

Schneider, too, had adopted more informal dress, and he too was working with a will, polishing brass rods, adjusting pipes and fittings, and constantly making notes on what he discovered as he worked.

It was, perhaps, the middle of the morning (I had left my watch at my apartment, fearing for its safety) when we perceived a knock at the door.

"I paid that man Gérard enough money to stay away, did I not?" explained Schneider in a state of some irritation. "Will you see who is knocking, and send them away, Gauthier? I am in the middle of some complex measurements here and do not wish to be interrupted."

I wiped my oily hands on a rag, and set off down the stairs. On opening the door, I beheld Agathe. It was not entirely a surprise to me, given that I had requested her presence, but I was not prepared for her to arrive so early.

"You appear fatigued," I told her. "I was not expecting you to come here at this early hour."

She smiled in reply as she took in my dishevelled and unkempt appearance. "Why, M. Gauthier," she laughed. "Have you taken up a new profession? Does whatever you are doing to put you in that condition really pay you better than writing for that magazine?"

"By no means," I said. "As I told you yesterday, Professor Schneider and I are busy cleaning and preparing the machinery that was discovered here, which corresponds to that which I saw in your father's laboratory."

"Show me!" she commanded, her eyes gleaming.

"It is dirty. I fear for your fine clothes." As I said these words, I was suddenly aware that her garments were not of the quality with which I usually associated her.

At this, she laughed outright. "My dear Jules, your concerns should be for me, rather than for my clothes, should they not? See," and with this, she spun around, showing that her garments were indeed those of a servant used to performing the most menial of domestic tasks. "Lead me. I am ready for all the dirt and grime that you can summon."

I had no option but to lead the way up the stairs, and take her to the room where Professor Schneider was still hard at work. He started when he saw Agathe.

"My dear Gauthier," he said to me. "I am aware that you dislike this work, but there is no call whatsoever for you to shirk it, and to pass it over to a common maid, who is almost certainly likely to cause some catastrophe in her ignorance as she attempts to clean this delicate mechanism."

I was mortified by his failure to recognise Agathe as a young lady of breeding, and looked over to her to see how she would react to this *gaffe*. To my surprise, she was smiling quietly, and showed no inclination to correct his mistake, clearly waiting for my intervention.

"Professor Schneider," I began hesitantly, "I fear that you are unaware of this young lady's identity." He looked up, and regarded me, and then Agathe, with some interest. "May I introduce Mademoiselle Agathe Lamartine, the daughter of Professor Lamartine?"

Confusion spread over the Professor's bear-like face as he realised the implications of my words. "My dear young lady... Mademoiselle... I am so sorry... your dress..."

"There is nothing for which you need apologise," she told him. "I am fully aware that my dress could cause confusion if it were the only criterion by which I am judged."

"Thank you, Mademoiselle. But," as a thought seemed to strike him, "may I ask what you are doing here? How did you come to know of this place? Who sent you here? What is your purpose in being here?" His voice rose in pitch and intensity with each question.

I decided that these were questions best answered by me. "She is here at my invitation, Professor. I trust Mademoiselle Lamartine absolutely. We met last night, and I told her about her father, and about this discovery here." Here Schneider let out a most undignified snort. "I asked her to search in her father's study for any papers relating to the Untime."

"And has she brought them? Have you?" he accused, turning on her.

"Indeed I have, Professor Schneider," she answered meekly, bringing a folded sheaf of papers from her bosom, and passing them to me. The warmth of her body was still on the papers as they rested in my hand, and despite myself, I trembled at the indirect intimacy. I had no doubt that her perfume also still remained on them, but I was not about to put this to the test in front of others, but merely handed the papers in my turn to Schneider, who took them, placed his pince-nez on his nose, and riffled through them.

"Where did you find these?" he enquired sharply of Agathe, looking up.

"They were in a drawer in the desk in his study," she answered him.

"Was the drawer locked?"

She turned red and stammered. "Yes. Yes, it was. I had a spare key with which I opened the lock."

"Is this relevant?" I asked Schneider.

"Indeed it is. Professor Lamartine is well aware of what you know, Gauthier, and it is not impossible that he might leave some papers containing false information in a prominent position hoping that they might be discovered, and thereby put the discoverer on a false trail. If, however, these papers were in a locked drawer, this possibility becomes less likely." He returned to the papers, and studied them intently. "It is excellent stuff as far as it goes," he told us, "but it does not go far enough, I fear. Some vital conclusions are missing."

"Perhaps these would help?" suggested Agathe, proffering another set of papers. I had not seen from where she had produced these, but Schneider did not seem to be concerned with their immediate provenance, merely taking the papers with a brusque word of thanks.

"Where were these discovered, then?" he asked.

"In his laboratory," she said. Schneider smiled a strange smile that I was unable to comprehend.

I drew in my breath. "I warned you, did I not, Agathe, that you should never go there."

"I took every precaution. I went to the laboratory. There was no sign of him there." Once again, Schneider gave what can only be described as a snort at these words. "I took these papers from his desk in the laboratory," she added. "The Professor, my father, that is, had given me a key to the laboratory, in case I ever took a fancy to perform my own experiments," she added by way of explanation.

"Your experiments?" I exclaimed. This was the first I had ever heard of Agathe's interest in such things.

"Why are you so surprised that the child of a scientist should follow her father?"

"Nothing, except that you..." my voice tailed off.

"...that I am a woman? Well, why should a woman not engage herself in the sciences? There is a woman from Poland who has recently married a Frenchman, Pierre Curie, and is making great progress in her field, discovering new elements, I am told. Why should I not do the same?"

I regarded Agathe with a new respect. I had never before encountered such a person, and her words astounded me.

Schneider, however, appeared to take the news in his stride. "And I take it that your father was not in his laboratory?"

"Obviously not, or I would not have these papers,"

she replied. "Indeed, there has been no sign of him anywhere for several days. He informed us that he had gone to Brest to hold discussions with the naval officers there, and these were of such a secret nature that we were not to attempt to communicate with him."

Schneider gave another of his inscrutable smiles. "And when you entered the laboratory, you saw the machine there, similar to this one here, that Gauthier here has described to me?" he asked.

"Indeed so, and it is almost identical, as far as I can tell on this first inspection," she said.

Schneider made a grunting sound, and resumed his perusal of the papers.

"There is an error here," he said, looking up. "One that could lead your father, Mademoiselle, into more dangerous paths than those of which he is currently aware?"

"What might that be?"

"I believe, after reading these notes, that Professor Lamartine is under the impression that he can use the Untime to go back in time and change history."

"But that would surely be a good thing? If the wrongs and evils of the past could be corrected?"

"It would indeed, if it were possible," replied Schneider. "But sadly, it is impossible." He shook his head.

Chapter XX

"**B**UT if we can go back in time, we can have an effect on what happens there, can we not?" I asked.

"You cannot change history," Schneider said to us. "To admit such a thing was possible would be to admit that many different histories exist."

"Why do they not?" I asked him. "For example, if I were to return to 1792 and rescue the King from the guillotine?"

"You could not do such a thing," he replied to me, shaking his head. "Something would prevent you from doing so."

"What would prevent me?"

"I cannot tell you exactly what it would be that would prevent you, but circumstances would prevail in such a way that you would be unable to accomplish your goal. You would be prevented somehow. Maybe you would break your leg on the way to the Tuileries for your rescue attempt, or you would be stopped by a guard. It is impossible to say exactly how events would transpire. The history you know, and that you will always know, is that on September 21, 1792, Louis XVI of France was executed by the guillotine. Nothing you can do in the Untime will change that fact.

"However," he continued, speaking as if he were delivering a lecture to his students at the Sorbonne, "if we accept the possibility of a number of univers- es, such as I described earlier, then it might be that in a different universe, we would now be living in the reign of Louis XX, whose family had reigned in an unbroken line for the past hundred years."

"I cannot believe this," said Agathe. "I refuse to be- lieve in your multiple universes." She seized a pen and began to scribble mathematical equations on a sheet of paper that lay to hand. I was completely unable to comprehend their meaning, and watched dumbfounded as the symbols continued to appear on the page as Agathe wrote, seemingly totally en- grossed in her calculations. At length, she put down the pen, and passed the paper to Schneider, who took it and glanced at it casually. His eyes were still fixed on it as he laid it aside on the table, but sud- denly his manner changed.

He picked up the paper once more, and scanned it, obviously giving it his full attention, running his finger down the line of equations. When he had reached the bottom of the paper, his finger returned to the top, and he repeated the operation, at a slower pace. His lips moved silently as he traced the math- ematics, and the process took a good three or four minutes.

At length he laid the paper aside once again, and sat in silence for a few minutes more. Eventually, he spoke.

"My sincere congratulations, Mademoiselle," he said, in a tone which was unlike his usual rough accents. "You are undoubtedly your father's daughter, and I would venture to suggest that your mental prowess exceeds his." He scribbled a couple of lines at the bottom of the paper, and passed it back to her.

She took the proffered paper, and scanned the additions, shaking her head. "No, no," she murmured, using the pen to amend his writing before returning the paper to him.

He scanned it once more, muttering to himself, and then looked up at her, gazing into her eyes. "My hat is off to you," he declared. He sketched the motion of doffing an imaginary cap with an exaggerated motion, and Agathe flushed.

"You mean, sir, that my little effort—"

"'Little effort' be damned!" thundered Schneider in his customary tones, clearly temporarily oblivious of the fact that he was addressing a member of the fair sex. "Your 'little effort' has completely overturned my theory in a matter of minutes. I cannot recall when I have seen such an argument so clearly and concisely expressed. I would ask one favour of you, Mademoiselle."

"What is that?"

"That you do not publish this work and my feeble attempts at criticism. It would make me a laughing stock throughout the world. Have no fear, though. I am not one of those who takes the work of others and passes it off as their own. I would simply ask you to keep this in the private eye for some time. May I beseech you to do this?"

"Of course, Professor," my Agathe replied, a merry twinkle in her eye, "if this really means so much to you."

"It does indeed mean much to me, and I thank you sincerely for your generosity of spirit in this matter," he answered her.

"Does this theory of Mlle. Lamartine disprove your thesis that we cannot change the past?" I asked. I was well aware that the mathematical reasoning that had just passed between the two was as incomprehensible to me as the workings of a steam-engine would be to an orang-utan, but I wished to have some explanation regarding its significance.

"By no means," he said. "By no means. It strengthens my conviction that we have one past and one past only. It does, however, somewhat work against my previous idea regarding a multiplicity of universes. Indeed, it completely invalidates it." He spoke with a rueful smile, which he turned on Agathe. "I promise you that there is a position for you to teach at the Sorbonne, should you ever desire it. I swear to you that, should you decide to take that course, I will do all in my power to smooth your path."

"Thank you, sir," she replied, with an admirable modesty of demeanour.

However, the task before us was not to engage in flights of philosophical fancy, but consisted merely of the mundane cleaning of the apparatus before us.

Such an occupation, though demanding physically at times, made few demands on my mental faculties, and I was therefore able to ponder on the exchange that had just taken place between my two companions. I was unable, naturally, to appreciate the finer points of the mathematics that my Agathe (as I now, perhaps somewhat prematurely, mentally referred to her) had placed before Schneider, but I was now able to understand, to my relief, that both she and Schneider considered our universe to be the only one in existence. More immediately as far as my heart was concerned, however, was the thought that the girl with whom I found myself in love (for this was not a conscious decision on my part) was the equal, if not the superior, of one of the foremost savants in France, at least in the field of theoretical mathematics. The prospect of an alliance with such a powerful intellect would give any man pause for thought, I told myself, and I vainly tried to disabuse myself of the idea that there was any mutual attraction between us.

This attempt was not assisted by the smiles and words of encouragement that came my way from Agathe at regular intervals as we worked together polishing the brass-work and glass of the apparatus, and cleaning the wooden bars of the framework. While we were doing this, Professor Schneider was engaged in tightening valves and re-filling the tanks and reservoirs that held the mysterious liquids and gasses which he had brought from his laboratory.

A thought struck me, and I attracted Schneider's attention. "We are cleaning this apparatus, are we not, and placing it in working order?"

"Of course, you fool," he exclaimed testily. "What else?"

"For what reason?"

"Surely it is obvious to you?" He smiled, but the expression on his face was not a pleasant one.

"So that Professor Lamartine can return here using it?"

"For Heaven's sake, man," protested Schneider, and the tone of his voice was angry. "You do not believe that Lamartine needs this to come back here? You told me yourself that in this Untime, you could roam at will through time and space?"

"I did."

"We have no idea when or where he will choose to come back to us. I think we may be certain that it will be soon. But where?" He spread his hands in an expressive gesture. "It could be anywhere in this world. I would be extremely surprised if it were in this house."

"But, then....?"

Agathe interrupted me. "What Professor Schneider means, Jules, is that if we cannot find my father in the normal time and space that we inhabit, then the Untime is where we must search for him."

"But you cannot do that, my dear, and Professor Schneider cannot..." My voice trailed off as I realised my two companions were looking at me.

Chapter XXI

"Y OU wish me to go into the Untime to discover his whereabouts?" I stammered.

"I would have thought that was obvious,"
replied Schneider in a somewhat sarcastic tone.

In a little gentler voice, my Agathe added, "Jules, you must understand that neither Professor
Schneider nor I has ever been into this Untime. It
was strange, you say?"

"Monstrously so," I answered her, surprising myself with my choice of word.

"But you, my dear, are the only man other than
my father to have experienced this strange state. If
either Professor Schneider or I should enter it—"

"God forbid, Agathe, that you should expose yourself to the Untime!"

"And you said yourself, did you not, Gauthier, that
I was unsuitable to enter the Untime?" Schneider
reminded me. To my horror, I confessed that this
was so. "In that case," Schneider went on, smiling
the sweet smile of a devil, "you are the only one of

our little company who is suited to take this voyage."

"Do you suppose that I can locate your father in the Untime?" I asked Agathe.

"From what you have told me, that is exactly what you did on the past occasion."

"And then what am I expected to do once he has been found?"

"You must stop him returning," said Schneider. "At least, you must stop him returning with his ideas about ruling our world."

"Do you think I can persuade him?" I was doubtful of my ability to do any such thing at the best of times, let alone in the Untime. "You must remember that we are talking of a man who had threatened me with a revolver and had sworn to hunt me down and kill me if I crossed his path."

"If you cannot persuade him, you must stop him and prevent him from causing any mischief," Schneider told me. I could hear Agathe catch her breath.

"You mean that Jules must kill my father?"

Schneider nodded his great bear-like head. "But only as a last resort. Consider, Mademoiselle. You have proved to me that you have a sound head on your shoulders. Should your father be unaware of the consequences of the equations that you produced so admirably earlier, what is the conclusion?"

I could see her turning the matter over in her mind, and suddenly visibly stop short and turn pale. "It would be the end of the world," she whispered hoarsely. "If not the end of the Universe as we know it."

"And what is one man's life against that?" Schneider demanded of her. "Even when that one man is your father?"

Agathe bit her trembling lip. "You are correct, *maître*, but you cannot expect me to dance with joy when I hear you say this."

"Be brave, my dear," I told her, placing a hand lightly on her shoulder. However, she shrugged off my hand with a twist of her body, and walked away from Schneider and me to the other side of the room, by the window.

"It is hard for me to accept in my heart what you say, Professor," she said to Schneider, "though my head acknowledges the truth of your words. Poor father. Poor Jules," she added, looking at me, and then broke into sobs. "No, do not touch me," she said, as I moved to comfort her. I looked over at Schneider, who merely raised his eyebrows and glanced at the apparatus that we had been cleaning.

I took the hint, picking up one of the rags we used for polishing the brass rods, and left Agathe to her weeping, though it nearly broke my heart to see her in that state of distress.

After a few minutes, her sobs stopped. "I am going out for a few minutes," she informed us. "I am sure you two men will have plenty to discuss." And, with a toss of her curls, she was gone.

"Women!" exclaimed Schneider. "Even the best of them, such as she, seem to be incapable of rational thought at times of crisis."

"I hardly think you are being fair to Mademoiselle Lamartine," I retorted. "You have just informed her that a young man for whom she has displayed some partiality is to take the life of her beloved father. May I turn the tables on you, Professor, and ask you exactly what would be your reaction under similar circumstances?"

"Impertinence!" he replied gruffly. "I shall not dignify such an enquiry with an answer." With that, he turned once more to the mechanism, and made several seemingly unnecessary adjustments to one of the numberless valves and stopcocks.

Not a word passed between us for some fifteen minutes, during which time we worked diligently at the restoration of the apparatus. The door opened, and Agathe entered the room.

"I have considered what you said, Professor," she addressed Schneider. "Of course you are right in saying that my father must be stopped from his meddling, and that the best way of achieving this is to meet him in the Untime. However, I am in complete disagreement as to both the means and the agency by which this shall be accomplished."

Schneider laid down the tools with which he had been working, and regarded her gravely. "Pray continue," he invited her.

"First, I think it is only natural on my part for me to express the wish that my father's life be spared, if this is at all possible. If persuasion, rather than force, can be used, I would find this to be infinitely preferable."

Schneider nodded. "I quite understand, Mademoiselle."

"And so," she continued, "I feel that it would not be wise to undertake to send M. Gauthier here to undertake the mission. Jules, you told me that my father threatened you, did you not?"

"Yes, that is correct."

"Do either of you think that he would be persuaded by M. Gauthier, charming and clever with words though he may be, rather than his own flesh and blood – myself?" she declaimed.

"You make an excellent point, Mademoiselle," replied Schneider.

He seemed poised to say more, but before he could utter a sound, I leaped into the discussion. "Agathe!" I exclaimed with all the vigour of which I was capable, "you shall not enter the Untime! It cannot be!"

She laid a calming hand on my sleeve. "Why not, my dear Jules?" she asked, with a smile that would have melted the heart of a marble statue.

"It is an absurd idea," I answered, angrily. "You have no conception of the Untime, other than as a series of equations on a piece of paper. You would become completely disorientated were you to enter the Untime. And your constitution, Agathe. Consider your health and the risk, not only to your body, but to your mind. Why, Professor Schneider here has declared to me that entering the Untime can cause severe damage to one's mental faculties. Is that not so, Professor?"

To my horror, the wretch refused to support me in this assertion. "It is true, Gauthier, that I may have made a remark to that effect in the past. However, on reflection and further calculation, I have come to revise my opinion on the matter. It is now my opinion that no harm will result to Mademoiselle Lamartine from a trip to the Untime."

I could cheerfully have put my hands around the Professor's throat and throttled him on the spot, had it not been for the presence of Agathe, which stayed my hand. It was she who broke the silence.

"I do confess that I feel more than a little nervous at the prospect of entering the Untime, and therefore I was going to suggest, before he so gallantly intervened on my behalf, that M. Gauthier accompanied me. That is to say, that the two of us enter the Untime together."

At these words, I felt a weight was lifted from my mind. It would be I, Jules Gauthier, who would be the protector of this remarkable woman whom I loved, and it would be I who would be her guide through the mysteries of those strange dimensions revealed by her father. My heart lifted as I considered the prospect, and I clasped her hand and lifted it to my lips.

"Together, my darling," I exclaimed in my passion. "We will conquer the Untime together!"

Chapter XXII

OTWITHSTANDING this determination, it was clear that more work needed to be done before Agathe and I could enter the Untime. Schneider reminded us both that there were many chemicals and liquids which were still necessary for the machinery to function properly, and he also gave it as his opinion that we had little time to spare before Lamartine reappeared in our time once more. This was a signal to us to work hard on the reconstruction of the apparatus, and we applied ourselves to the task to such good effect that Schneider pronounced the machine to be in working order the very day after the conversation recorded above.

"You must test it," I told him. "Take a watch or some such and send it forward in time by an hour or so." I offered my own timepiece for the purpose.

"I suppose that is a wise precaution," he admitted, taking the watch. "I feel I have sufficient knowledge of the way in which the controls work."

He placed the watch in the centre of the glass plate

and bent to the control panel.

"When Professor Lamartine performed this experiment in front of me," I reminded him, "we required dark goggles, and stopped our ears with cotton-wool. Remember that this operation will produce a considerable flash and noise. We would also do well to cover the windows, so that we do not attract the attention of the neighbours."

"Very well," he said. "Do we have any such goggles here? I have seen none."

"Nor I," I replied.

It was Agathe who discovered two sets of goggles in a bureau drawer, with the lenses constructed from smoked glass. I was more than happy to allow her and Schneider to be the witnesses of the disappearance, my eyes and ears having suffered from such an event in the past. However, I gave both Agathe and Schneider due warning, which they took under advisement, and we proceeded to hang the heavy drapes over the windows once more, as they had been when I first entered the room several days previously. I watched my beloved and Schneider fill their ears with some balls of the cotton waste, taken from the supply that we had acquired for wiping down the machine, and adjust the goggles over their heads. I waved a farewell with my hand, and stepped down the stairs and into the street.

After I had been waiting for about a minute, a loud report issued from the house. A horse pulling a carriage shied, and it was necessary for the driver to calm him, but otherwise there was no other reaction that I could observe, from the neighbours or from any passer-by. I re-entered the house and mounted the stairs to find Agathe collapsed in a chair, with Professor Schneider standing over her, fanning her face with a sheet of paper. A glance at the apparatus was enough to show me that the watch had vanished.

"The poor girl was overcome by the noise and the flash," he told me. "To be frank with you, it took me by surprise, even though you had warned us of the intensity of the event. I have removed her goggles, as you can see, but her eyes remain closed."

I poured a glass of mineral water from the bottles with which the Professor and I had provided ourselves, and held it to her lips. With her eyes still closed, she accepted a few sips of water, and then opened her eyes and looked me in the eye.

"How are you, my dear?" I asked her, but received no reply other than a look of incomprehension. "She has been deafened by the violence of the explosion!" I cried, but happily it transpired that I was mistaken in my assumption. My Agathe smiled sweetly at me, and raised her hands to her ears, whence she drew the balls of cotton waste that had plugged them.

"Now what was it you were saying to me just now, Jules?" she asked, with that sweet but impudent smile on her face.

"I was asking if you were well," I laughed. "But it appears that my enquiry is a little superfluous."

"Thank you, but I am now quite well and recovered. However, the noise of the explosion was more than I was expecting, and I am afraid I must have lost my senses."

"Are you sure that you will be able to travel to the Untime and survive its rigours?" I asked her.

"I can only tell you that I will do my utmost." The look on her face was one of determination, and was enough to convince me of her intent.

"How long until the watch re-appears?" I asked the Professor.

"I set the time for approximately thirty minutes from now," he informed me. "Mademoiselle
Lamartine assisted me in this, and though we are not
completely familiar with the workings of the mechanism, I can express with reasonable confidence that
the setting is tolerably accurate. We have now another," he pulled a large watch from his pocket, "twen-
ty-three minutes to wait. I suggest that we spend the
time in settling what objects you should take with
you into the Untime."

I laughed in his face. "My dear Professor Schneider,"
I told him. "In the Untime, one is totally unconscious
of one's body. There is no way in which any physical
object would be of any use there. The only thing that
I might recommend," I added, remembering my own
experience, "would be a small bottle of *eau de vie* or
something similar. There is something in the Untime
that saps the heat from one's body on returning to
our dimensions."

"That may well be so," said Schneider. "However, it
would seem prudent to be prepared for any eventuality when you leave the Untime, at whatever time or
place you may find yourself."

Again, I laughed. "The place may be the North Pole
or the middle of the Sahara desert. And the time?
That may be the present day, or it may be the Middle
Ages or the Classical Age of the Greeks. Or it may be
a time in the future, when the whole world is ruled
by electrical devices, and humanity is no more than
a redundant cog in the world's machinery."

"What a poetic turn of phrase you have, to be
sure," smiled Agathe. "But then, I suppose that is
your trade."

"My point, all poetry aside," I went on, "is that to
be sure of being prepared for any eventuality, one

would need to carry a vast trunk, crammed with every contrivance known to man."

"At least let me persuade you to take this on your travels," answered the Professor, reaching inside his coat and withdrawing a large, heavy revolver, at the sight of which Agathe let out a little involuntary shriek of fear.

"You would want Jules here to use this against my father?" she exclaimed.

"I sincerely hope that it will prove unnecessary," he answered her. "However, I believe it behoves him and you to be well prepared for any eventuality. If what I have been told, and what my own calculations tell me are correct, then there is no knowing what you may encounter in the Untime."

"You are beginning to give me even more cause for alarm," said Agathe. "To what sort of things are you referring?"

"Given the infinite nature of Space, and the eternal nature of Time, it could be anything? From the monstrous lizards that roamed the Earth in ancient times, to such creatures as may inhabit the most distant planets in our Universe, and of which we can have no conception as to their nature."

I laughed. "In that case, my dear Professor Schneider," I retorted, returning the weapon to him, "I hardly think that such a crude physical weapon such as a revolver will be of any assistance to us in our travels. In any event, suppose that we do leave the Untime to enter the frozen wastes of Siberia or the steaming jungles of the Amazon, whether in our own time, or at any time in the past or the future, we will have no way of returning to the Untime, and hence to Paris. What must be done, must be done in the Untime, and there is therefore no need for us to carry such a weapon. Furthermore, did I not mention to you earlier, if I am not mistaken, that Professor Lamartine and I were careful to remove all metal from our persons before entering the Untime? I hardly wish to risk entering it carrying that monstrosity," and I indicated the pistol.

Schneider appeared to be a little discomfited by my refusal, but accepted my argument, albeit with what appeared to be bad grace.

"In that case, since you seem determined to set off unprepared and defenceless, I would suggest that you start as soon as the watch reappears, which will be in approximately three minutes from now."

Almost as he finished speaking, the watch appeared on the glass plate, and I went to pick it up, noting the time. "Indeed, it is at the same time as when it left us," I said.

"Although the machinery appears to be slightly imperfectly adjusted," said Schneider, "as can be seen from the early appearance of the watch, this should make no difference to animate sentient beings such as yourself and Mademoiselle Lamartine. It is time for you to take your places. Remove all metal from your persons."

Chapter XXIII

HAVING divested myself of all metal objects, and Agathe having done the same, she and I took our place on the glass plate which stood at the centre of the machinery.

"Hold my hand, Jules," she said softly to me. "I do not consider myself a coward, but I need the reassurance of your presence. I took her small, cool, dry hand in mine, uncomfortably aware of the fact that my own palm was moist with anxiety.

Although I had undergone this experience in the past, I still felt considerable trepidation as I watched Professor Schneider approach the control panel. After all, I reasoned, he was not the inventor of the machine, and his understanding of the principles governing it, though far in advance of my own, was far from perfect, as was shown by the way in which the watch had returned to us somewhat earlier than we had expected.

As before, there was an uncomfortable feeling that my body had disappeared. The choking sensation

and the heat that I had experienced on the previous
occasion were also very much in evidence, and I experienced considerable discomfort once again, but
as before, this passed quite quickly. I was intensely
aware of the presence of Agathe beside me, but the
pressure of her hand in mine had disappeared, as
indeed had her hand itself, and mine.

Though I had no head to turn, it seemed, nonetheless I could direct my attention in a particular
direction, and though all that I could perceive was
the same pale green glow that had accompanied me
on my previous visit to the Untime, I was very much
aware of Agathe's presence. This was in contrast to
the previous occasion, when I had not been aware of
the presence of her father without a conscious effort
on my part to detect it.

Although, as I say, nothing was visible, Agathe still
seemed to me as an invisible luminous presence. I
realise that what I have just set down is a contradiction in terms, and that you will write me down as a
madman for these words, but it is the closest that I
can come to explaining myself here.

I remembered the method by which I had been
able to communicate with Professor Lamartine previously, and adjusted my mind in an attempt to make
contact with Agathe. Almost immediately, her un-
heard words filled my head. You must realise that
when we were communicating with each other in
the Untime in this way, although no words were au-
dible, it was still very possible to distinguish tone
of voice and so on, and on this occasion, it was in a
much clearer fashion than had been the case with
Agathe's father and myself previously.

I had occasion to speak confidentially at a later
date with an English savant specialising in psychic

matters, and he gave it as his considered belief that the affection that was present between Agathe and myself was the cause of this improved link between our souls in the Untime.

"It is magnificent!" she exclaimed. Certainly, there seemed to be no trepidation in her voice, and there was a confidence there that, quite frankly, I envied. "It is extraordinary, Jules," she continued. "I can see nothing but this pale mist that surrounds me, but at the same time, I am fully conscious of your presence, and of your voice inside me. How exciting this all is!"

I could not help but admire her spirit and her attitude. I had been fully prepared to act as her guide and support, should she fall prey to the terrors of the Untime, but it now appeared to me that I might well be the one supported, given her seemingly indomitable nature.

"I am beginning to understand," she went on, "the megalomania that afflicted my dear father."

"I hope that this is not going to affect you also," I replied.

There was the delicious sound of a chuckle inside my mind. "My dear Jules, I sincerely trust that you do not believe me to be subject to these same temptations."

"By no means," I assured her.

"Very well, then. I have the strong impression that a single step will take us anywhere in the Universe, simply by willing it to be so. Is that your understanding?"

"That is what I believe."

"Very good, then. My study of my father's papers, and my own mathematical calculations also, have persuaded me of this. I have always entertained a fancy to see a kangaroo in its natural habitat. Shall

we take a brief stroll together to Australia, my dear
Jules?" There was something between delight and
mockery in the way that her words resounded, which
I found entrancing.

"With all my heart," I responded, in the same vein,
and together we took the two steps that brought us
to the edge of the Australian desert. Naturally, we did
not leave the Untime, for we would have had no way
of re-entering, but it was possible for us to observe
the arid landscape, albeit through a faint green haze.
In the distance, it was possible to discern some of
the marsupials about which Agathe had expressed
her interest. Not ten metres in front of us was a family of the Aboriginal inhabitants of the place, consisting of a mother, a father, and two small children, one
of whom was being carried on his mother's back.
Although his back was turned to us, the little mite
seemed aware of our presence, and turned his head
towards us, looking straight into my eyes, though I
assumed that we were invisible to the little fellow,
since there was no recognition in his face, rather
there was simply a fixed fascination. His mother became aware of his attention, and turned to face us.
Soon the whole family was staring fixedly in our direction, but apparently without being able to see us.

Without warning, the father of the family seized
his long wooden spear and hurled it directly at me.
If I had been physically present, it would, I judged,
have struck me in the chest, but in the Untime, it
merely passed insensibly straight through me.

I sensed a gasp from Agathe. "Are you hurt?" I
heard.

"Not at all," I sent back to her. "There was no feeling at all."

"I think it is time for us to go," her words echoed

in my head.

We took ourselves back into the middle of the Untime, where the pale green mist enveloped us once more.

"Do you think," Agathe asked me, " that we are appearing as ghosts or spirits to those people?"

"I am not sure that we are actually appearing," I answered her, "but it seems to me that the general reaction is that which some people describe when they describe seeing a ghost. Where would you like to go next, my dear?"

"It is not where I would like to go next, but when. Can we step backward and forward in time as easily as we did through space just now? Please do reassure me of this, as I have no wish to be trapped in some time where there is no escape."

"I know from experience that it is possible to travel forward in time," I told her. I see no reason why it should not be as easy to travel backward, provided always that we stay within the Untime, and do not leave the green that surrounds us."

"Green?" came her question. "But it is pink, surely? You are not colour-blind, are you?"

I was able to assure her categorically that I did not suffer from that condition, having recently taken a test as part of the research for an article I was writing on the subject. "But what time would you like to visit?" I asked.

Her answer astonished me. "I would like to visit Ancient Egypt at the time of Cleopatra. Her story has always fascinated me, that she was able to entrance and seduce the most powerful men in the world at that time, and that, it is said, without being beautiful."

"I hope that you are not intending to make her

your model," I laughed.

"Indeed not. Humour my womanly fantasy, if you would, though, my dear Jules."

Again, I lack the words to describe how we navigated our way through the centuries to the court of Cleopatra, as she entertained the great Roman general Marcus Antonius. We remained within our coloured mists, apparently out of sight behind a pillar in the throne room.

Chapter XXIV

ERE, as an aside, I wish to set down one of the strangest parts of our adventure in the Untime, which has little or no bearing on the story that I am relating, but it seems to me on reflection that it would be remiss of me not to report it to you. I have explained previously that Time and space were fluid in the Untime, and that moving around in these dimensions was a trivial affair, no matter what the distance or time involved. However, there was yet another dimension, if so it may be termed, of which I was not aware when we entered the Untime, and whose existence I still find it hard to credit, even after I have experienced it at first hand. If my words and my description here seem a little incoherent, please forgive me. I am, to my knowledge, the only man, and one of only two people in this world to have undergone this experience, and it was so extraordinary that mere words have failed me in attempting to describe it and its effect on me.

This dimension is the one of gender. Incredible as

it may seem, in the Untime, it was possible for me
to change gender at will, and I became aware of this
very shortly after I entered the Untime with Agathe,
before we made our journey to Australia. I have a
suspicion, which, of course, it is impossible for me to
verify or disprove, that it was the presence of Agathe
in the Untime with me which provided me with this
awareness, and possibly also facilitated the process
of change. Of course, my first visit to the Untime
was made in the company of Professor Lamartine,
another man, and one to whom I felt no emotional
attachment, but it is possible that I am making as-
sumptions here that cannot be justified.

Of course, in the Untime, one is bodiless, and it
was not possible for me to know whether such a
change in my gender was mental only, or whether it would be reflected in my physical appearance
should I choose to leave the Untime. I confess that
I was most unwilling to make the experiment, quite
apart from the difficulty of returning to the Untime
should I leave it, and therefore am unable to inform
you of the probable result in this regard, should you
by some chance in the future find yourself able to
visit the Untime, and wish to undertake this change.

While we were finding our feet in the Untime,
so to speak, Agathe and I were able to communicate with each other, as I mentioned, and I was able
to inform her, phrasing the matter as delicately as
possible, of what I had discovered, and what I had
achieved. She showed her mettle and her qualities
as an explorer of the unknown, and immediately decided for herself that she wished to experiment with
this new dimension. Like me, she was unwilling to
take herself out of the Untime in her changed state,
but was happy to explore the feelings and emotions

of a different gender.

As far as the purely mental side of changing gender is concerned, I am able to report that the experience was unlike anything else I have experienced. For those who claim that the differences between men and women are merely those that relate to bodily appearance, I can only reply that you have no conception of the true state of things. My thoughts in my female self took on a new resonance and depth that were unique in my experience. I found myself in tune with the universe on a different level from that I had previously experienced. My sympathy and empathy with all things appeared to be enhanced, and I found myself more deeply engaged with everything around me. It was easier for me to relate to matters outside myself, insofar as I was able to consider them while I was in the Untime, and I gained a different kind of understanding to that which I was accustomed.

At the same time, various aspects of my personality that I had not previously regarded as being exclusively masculine disappeared from my perspective. The barriers that my mind had thrown up over the years to protect me against the slings and arrows of fortune seemed to be weaker, and I felt more vulnerable to those aspects of the world that seemed to oppress me or to be out of tune with my interests. I began to understand some of the feelings in women that men classify as emotional fragility. Even so, if I am to be frank, I enjoyed the sensations that these female sensations produced in me.

I felt a little less happy, though, at the loss of my masculine armour. I cannot honestly say that I found the experience of this loss to be altogether pleasant, as some of those characteristics by which I usual-

ly define and differentiate myself from others had
also disappeared, or so it seemed to me, since they
were so bound up with the masculine image which I
present to the world. As with so many aspects of the
Untime, it is almost impossible to express the whole
of the experience and the feelings that it aroused in
mere words, but this changing of my gender is one
that I will never forget, and which I am immensely
grateful to have undergone, though I know that I will
never enter the Untime again. However, while I was
undergoing this experience, though so many of the
sensations were pleasant, on an intellectual plane,
I found the concept to be jarring and unpleasing. I
was glad to return to my normal self, and to leave the
female version of my character behind, though if I
am to be honest, I would have to say that there are
times when I wish I could return to it.

After our adventure in the Untime, on comparing
notes with Agathe, I discovered that she had experienced much the same feelings as had I, but in re-
verse. She, too, had shed some aspects of her character which may be described as feminine, and had
gained other, masculine character traits. Like me,
she felt the loss of some of the characteristics of her
original gender, but considered others to be a gain.

Incidentally, we both noted a strange phenomenon. As I have mentioned, I believed the mist with
which we surrounded in the Untime as being green,
while Agathe reported its colour as being pink.
When I took on the female gender, it seemed to me
that the colour of the mist changed to pink, and then
reverted to green when I re-assumed the male gender. For Agathe, the situation was reversed – the mist
changed from pink to green and then back to pink.
Proof, if there be any who still doubt it, that men

and women do indeed perceive the world in different ways.

After discussing the whole of the matter at length (which we were only to do following our marriage, however) we admitted to each other that we were both happy to revert to our original genders within the Untime, a process which happily proved to be as easy as the initial change, but both of us might welcome the chance, should it be offered, to repeat the process at some time in the future – provided always that it was reversible.

This extraordinary experience, which, dare I say it, is almost certainly unique, has changed the life that Agathe and I live together. Each of us now possesses an understanding of each other which is denied to many couples who are not so fortunate as to have acquired such comprehension that comes with a change in gender, however temporary such a change may have been. If half the world were to gain the understanding of the other half that both Agathe and I encountered, I venture to suggest that the world would be a better and a happier place.

Chapter XXV

HEN we were standing in what appeared
to be Cleopatra's throne room, though
servants, almost certainly slaves, were very
much in evidence, there was no sign of the Queen,
or of her famous paramour. We could distinguish the
sound of trumpets and of drums beating a measured
cadence, which grew louder, as slaves bearing gold-
en symbols of royalty entered, followed by two litters
borne on the shoulders of enormous Nubian slaves.

These litters were placed on the ground, as the
trumpets blared a final discordant note, and two
maidservants opened the curtains of the first one.
Out of the litter stepped a scantily-dressed woman,
somewhat short and dumpy in appearance, with a
heavily painted face and black hair that was patently
a wig. As the assembled crowd fell to its knees and
bowed their heads, I realised that this somewhat un-
prepossessing woman making her way to the throne
must be the famous Cleopatra herself. It was not
clear to me at first sight how such a character could

ever have obtained the reputation of a great seduc-
tress. There was, nothing that I could discern, with
the eye of a lover of Agathe, that could compare in
any way with the charms of my beloved.

"Well, what do you think?" Agathe's words came
to me.

"I am astounded that her reputation that has come
down to us is what it is," I answered. However, as I
observed Cleopatra, I became aware of a seductive
aura that surrounded her movements and her person, and I was less sure of the words that I had just
spoken. "Let us now see what the famous Mark An-
tony has to show us."

As if on cue, the curtains of the second litter parted,
and a muscular masculine arm, wearing many gold-
en armbands, appeared in the gap. The arm was followed by the body of a man who must, in his prime,
have been a perfect Hercules, but now appeared as
a pitiful wreck. It was clear to my eye that he was
suffering from the effects of overindulgence in the
recent past, and that he was having difficulty making his way out of the litter. Two slaves approached
him, and offered their shoulders as support, but he
brushed them aside with massive sweeps of his arm,
swaying slightly on his feet as he did so.

He lifted his head, and I saw his face for the first
time. It was one of a man who was born to nobili-
ty and power, and who was used to command. That
much was clear, but at the same time, it was also
painfully obvious that this was a man who had been
ruined, either at his own hands, or at those of others,
who had exploited his weaknesses to bring him to
this present shameful condition.

He spoke in a language which was unknown to me,
and a slave approached him, running, and bearing

a jewelled goblet in one hand and a jug in another. Kneeling before Marcus Antonius (for this was indeed that tragic ruined figure), he poured dark wine into the goblet, which Antonius then seized and drained in one mighty draught, before holding it out to be refilled.

In the meantime, Cleopatra sat watching on her throne, a half-smile of cynical amusement on her face. She spoke a few words in what appeared to be the same tongue that Antonius had used earlier, and her face changed to a welcoming expression. As if mesmerised, Antonius started to lurch toward her, and this time he did not refuse the proffered assistance of the slaves.

Even so, as he reached the bottom step of the dais on which stood the throne, his foot slipped, and he fell heavily to the ground. As he reached for the waiting arms of the slaves, struggling to his feet, his face froze, and he turned his gaze, with an expression of terror upon his face, in the direction of Agathe and myself. He extended his left fist towards us with the index and little fingers extended, in a gesture that I recalled was intended by the ancient Romans to ward off evil, and slowly took hesitant steps in our direction, before bellowing something incomprehensible to the room at large.

Immediately there was a rustling and a commotion and all in the room reacted. Some produced jewelled amulets from within their garments, and some repeated in our direction the gesture that Antonius had made towards us. However, it did not seem that any of those had seen us, though some certainly appeared to be conscious of our presence.

The Queen gave an order, and a slave bowed low and ran from the chamber, while the court fluttered and fidgeted in an ecstasy of terror. Cleopatra herself seemed unmoved by the events around her, and sat calmly, even regally, on her throne as she surveyed the scene.

Marcus Antonius, for his part, was plainly in the grip of an almost paralysing fear. As had been the case with the Australian aboriginals, he plainly sensed our presence, but was unable to confirm it. It may well be that he regarded his perception of us as one of the effects of his love of wine, or some such, but in any event, our presence was obviously unwelcome to him.

Faint, almost inaudible, mutterings filled the throne room for the space of a few minutes. The near-silence was broken by the return of the slave who had been dispatched earlier.

He preceded an impressive personage, dressed in what appeared to be priestly robes, and followed by a number of slaves carrying mysterious impedimenta. He bowed low to Cleopatra, who addressed him in brusque tones, obviously commands.

At once, the slaves laid out their burdens, consisting of a low table and various gilded objects that they placed upon it. The priest faced the table, and pointed his staff in a direction that was nowhere near where we were located and started to chant, in a language different to that used by Cleopatra and Antonius.

The action seemed to raise Antonius to a rage. Seizing the unfortunate priest roughly by the shoulders, he spun the wretched man round to face us with such force that he nearly fell to the ground, and pointed accurately in our direction.

The priest, somewhat discomfited by this, raised his staff again, and continued his chanting. It was

clear to me that he, unlike Antonius, had no perception of our presence, and was merely going through
a form of words. Even so, I felt a strange, uncomfortable tingling sensation (though how this was possible in my incorporeal state, I cannot properly explain) and on communicating with Agathe, I learned
that she was also experiencing the same feelings.

In the meantime, Antonius continued to glare at
us with his bloodshot eyes, sipping continually from
the goblet which he still held, and which was being
constantly refilled by the slave standing by his elbow.

After about five minutes of chanting, the priest
lowered his staff, and turned to face Antonius, who
spoke to him in an angry tone, pointing once more
in our direction. The priest resumed his chanting,
and took two steps closer to us. The unpleasant tingling sensation became stronger, and I began to feel
that it would be wise for us to move from the place.

On letting Agathe know my feelings on the matter, I was not completely surprised to find her in
agreement.

"In any event," she communicated to me, "although
these tourist excursions to different times and places are fascinating, they are not the reason why we are
here. We must act to find my father, and to persuade
him away from his dreams of world domination."

"Of course," I agreed, and with one step, we were
back in the mists of the Untime, well away from
Cleopatra and her court.

"I suppose," remarked Agathe, "that we have just
been exorcised as ghosts or spirits." Her laughter
sounded inside my head.

"I suppose that is so," I agreed. "I wonder if our appearance and banishment is recorded in any historical documents? Is your curiosity now satisfied with

regard to Cleopatra, by the way?"

"Indeed it is. It is not for me to say, but I began to perceive why a certain type of man would find her attractive. Did you find her to your liking, Jules?"

I did not wish to answer this question, but instead suggested that we visit the future.

"Can we really see what life will be like in two hundred years?" she said.

"Come, my dear," I said, and we stepped forward to the year 2096.

Chapter XXVI

LTHOUGH we were enclosed by the faint green mist once more, the overwhelming impression of the future was one of greyness. We had moved ourselves in space to the Arc de Triomphe at the top of the Champs Elysées. The Arc itself stood above us, as imposing and as magnificent as always, but the expected view of Haussmann's grand avenues was missing.

Instead, we beheld soulless slabs of grey stone or concrete, towering to dizzying heights, and pierced by small windows, which could hardly have afforded any illumination to the inhabitants of these barracks.

It was natural for me to suppose that there would be fewer horses in this France of the future, but there were none at all in evidence. Instead, we were surrounded by a swirling stream of small vehicles, proceeding almost silently, but at a terrifying speed, propelled by their own mechanisms, perhaps using electricity, or perhaps steam, but it was impossible to tell from their appearance.

There were relatively few pedestrians, and those who were visible hurried along the pavements by the side of the road, dressed in brightly coloured clothing in a style that can only be described as immodest, with seemingly naked limbs very much in evidence. These garments formed the only splash of colour in the scene. The distant horizon was invisible behind a grey haze, and the sky was a leaden colour, unbroken by any shape of clouds, let alone a patch of blue sky.

"What has happened?" asked Agathe. "This must be Paris, but what a Paris it has become. It seems like a Hell on earth. Let us leave here and go to a more congenial spot, and discover what is happening elsewhere at this time."

I suggested Zermatt, a pleasant Swiss mountain resort where those who indulged in such things skated and skied on the snow. We soon found ourselves on a pleasant Alpine meadow, where to our relief, the blue sky was visible in places through the overcast.

I was enjoying the prospect, when Agathe interrupted my thoughts.

"Jules!" she exclaimed. "Where is the snow?"

"Why, it is—" and there I stopped. We had travelled to Zermatt in November, a time when the lower slopes of the Alps, not to mention the peaks, should be covered with snow. Instead, the area where we were standing, which should have been covered in a white blanket, was covered by a profusion of Alpine flowers. Not only that, but the peaks that towered above us were bare of snow.

"Are you sure we are in the right place, and that this is indeed November?" Agathe asked me, and her voice tailed off, as she knew she could answer the question for herself through the omniscience pro-

vided by the Untime. "What has happened, though?
What could possibly have made this change?"

As we stood pondering the matter, an animal came
into view at some distance from us, which I soon
discerned to be a camel. This extraordinary (for the
area) sight was followed by another such beast, and
another, and I was soon treated to the spectacle of a
caravan of camels progressing along a valley in the
Alps. Their handlers, who walked beside the beasts,
were equally unlikely inhabitants of the moun-
tains, resembling as they did Bedouins in dress and
appearance.

"What in the name of goodness is happening
here?" I asked.

"Let us return to Egypt, but the Egypt of this time,
not that of Cleopatra," she said. "If the Egyptians are
now living in Switzerland, who is living in Egypt?"

We took ourselves to the land of the Pyramids, and
were further stunned by our discoveries there. The
mighty Sphinx, which admittedly I had only seen in
illustrations and photographs, was almost completely covered by sand. There was no sign of any human
existence near the Pyramids, which must have been
likewise half-buried in the drifts, since they were nowhere near the size that I had been led to believe.

"Let us look at the Nile," suggested Agathe, and
we went to the river – or rather what had been the
mighty waterway, now reduced to a mere trickle, not
a metre wide, between what had presumably been
the banks of the river, but the outlines of which were
now, like all else, obscured by the sand. The city of
Cairo, when we explored further, was a ghost city,
likewise covered by sand, with only the tops of the
doors on the ground floors of the buildings visible
above the drifting dunes. The deserted minarets of

the mosques towered above us, silent witnesses to – what?

The sight was impressive and frightening. I did not know what was stranger and more repellent to me; the grey machine-like appearance of my beloved Paris, or this strange silent ruin of a great city, inhabited only by a few jackals, which we glimpsed in the distance, skulking between the buildings like silent ghosts.

Beside me, Agathe shuddered. "What has happened to our world, Jules?" she asked, and there was a tremor in her words. "What has caused this catastrophe?"

"I have no idea," I told her, and shuddered in my turn. "Let us go back into the Untime."

We turned away back into the formless green mist, when I suddenly became aware of another consciousness in the Untime. This was something inhuman, and one which produced an almost paralysing terror.

Chapter XXVII

ALTHOUGH we were without bodies, it seemed to me that Agathe clung to me as she and I simultaneously sensed the presence of this Other in the Untime.

"What is it?" were her words to me.

I was unable to answer this. My sensations were those of emotions, not of words, as they were with Agathe and had been with her father. The overriding impression that I gained from this Other was one of raw anger and hostility, which overwhelmed me, almost to the point of my losing consciousness. I could feel Agathe's mind beside me weakening under the onslaught, and I desperately fought to stay alert, for her sake.

"What are you? Who are you?" I thought in the direction of the Other. I had no way of knowing whether my words would be understood, or whether the Other was capable of replying, but I sent out the message time and time again, with all the intensity I could muster.

The reply came, but it was a reply of images, not of words, and I reeled from the shock. The picture that presented itself in my mind was one of a nightmare creature. It is a vision that haunts me still on the nights that I find myself unable to sleep, and I know that Agathe, too, still suffers from its memory, though she fell into a mental coma almost immediately after the Other revealed itself to us. I would say that she fainted, but the phrase would have little or no meaning when applied to our incorporeal state.

How can I begin to describe the horror that appeared before my mind's eye? It was a nightmare vision of innumerable tentacles and feelers, covered with a skin that appeared hideously wrinkled and coated with slime, writhing and squirming in a manner that was at once both obscene and fascinating. Behind this seething forest of glistening flesh shone a mass of dark eyes, similar to the eyes of a spider, as seen through a high-powered lens or microscope.

There was a mouth, too, framed by a massive hooked beak, which opened and closed, revealing in its black depths rows of serrated teeth, flecked with some nameless ichor that appeared to smoke and steam, and a long black serpent's tongue that constantly flicked back and forth, as though it had a mind and an existence of its own, independent of the horrific entity to which it was attached.

Two pairs of enormous bat-like wings soared above this monstrosity, beating slowly, though it was impossible to discern in what sort of atmosphere this creature had its being, and how it flew.

But, over and above the physical experience of this thing, the whole excited a kind of horror and disgust such as I have never experienced in the past, and never want to encounter again. This feeling was vis-

ceral in nature, and it was impossible for me to persuade myself that the vision before me was merely in
my mind, so strongly did it impress itself upon me.

Given the bizarre and horrifying nature of its fea-
tures, it was impossible to interpret any kind of facial
expression, but the anger and rage that I had first
discerned as emanating from it were, if anything,
stronger than before.

"What do you want?" I sent out to the Other, but
even as I did so, I knew the answer. This horror wanted us! Its meat and drink were the souls of those
who braved the Untime, whether they be human beings, or creatures from other worlds whose form and
being is unknown to us.

I laughed bitterly to myself at the thought of the
revolver that Professor Schneider had offered to
us before our departure into the Untime. What use
would such an instrument possibly be against a
monster of this kind? Even assuming that it had a
bodily physical existence, even the heaviest revolver
would be of little more use than a child's peashooter
when deployed against its massive form.

I now had to consider how I was to escape this
thing's terrible intentions. I had to assume that it
was as easy for it to travel through the Untime to
any point in space or time as it was for me to do the
same. If I were to leave the Untime, I would be faced
with the problem of returning to the same place and
time that I left. Space would be easy – I could, for
example, place myself in the middle of the Sahara
desert, or even the unexplored interior of the great
Antarctic continent, and hope that the beast would
follow me there. Once out of the Untime, I would
surely perish, either in the maw of this thing, or else
of heat and thirst induced by the desert, or cold,

should I choose the Antarctic. I would die, however, with the satisfaction of knowing that the beast would be incapable of surviving the harsh climate to which I had transported myself.

But... and there is always a but! I was in the Untime with Agathe, whose mind was currently closed to me, though I knew with certainty that she was still alive. If I were to take her with me to the desert or the frozen icy wastes, she would likewise die with me, which was a truly unimaginable prospect, and it was impossible for me to even consider leaving her alone in the Untime in her present condition.

Nor could I consider a temporal move through the Untime. Either to the past or the present, the monster could surely follow me as quickly and with the same facility as I myself moved. How would I return to my own time once I left the Untime? And, once again, Agathe's condition made it impossible for me to consider such a course of action.

The only practicable exit from the Untime was the house in Vincennes at the time when we had left it. That was likewise impossible for me to consider seriously, given that the monster would follow me out of the Untime into the world. Was I, even posthumously (as I surely would perish), to be known as the man who unleashed such a horror on the fair city of Paris? No, no, and a thousand times no!

My decision was made. I must stay in the Untime, and fight the horror with the only weapon at my disposal – my mind! Though I had little or no idea how I would achieve this, it came to me that my opponent, though large and of a fearsome aspect, possessed little in the way of mental faculties, and it was possible for me to defeat it with relatively little effort on my part.

Once again, I am using words in an attempt to describe a state and actions which were essentially non-verbal. If I sometimes use physical terms and expressions, I would ask you to remember that all this, though taking place in the mental realm alone, often had the same effect as physical sensations, including blows and attacks, with the resultant feelings of pain and agony. If my writing seems absurd to you as a result of this seeming contradiction, I crave your indulgence.

There was one other curious aspect to the monster, which alternately attracted and repelled me. How, I hear you ask, could I feel attraction to such a loathsome entity? The answer is through the power of scent.

I have never experienced the sense of smell in a dream, but the sensations I received from the Other in the Untime were almost overpowering. By turns, the monster emanated the sweetest scent imaginable; almost impossible to describe accurately, but the closest I can come is that my memory has it as the sweet odour of vanilla, mixed with that of roses. The smell was irresistibly seductive, and I found myself being drawn towards the monster without any conscious volition on my part, even while I shuddered at the horror of its source.

Alternating with this scent was a foul sewer stench, which initially I could perceive only fleetingly, but the more I gazed on the monster, the more prolonged the periods of this nauseating smell became, and the vanilla and roses dwindled away and became less and less frequent, until at length the only smell perceptible from the Other was that of filth and decay. All the attraction I had felt previously disappeared.

As I confronted the monster, it seemed to me to

be necessary to give my opponent a name. By naming one's fears, one is able to confront them and engage with them at a more intimate and deeper level than if they are simply nameless horrors. I therefore dubbed the monster "Dagon", and immediately I had done this, I felt a surge of power over my enemy.

Dagon attacked me with all the power of its mind, and I reeled under the shock. The closest thing to which I can compare it is as if I were being roasted by a jet of intense flame. But I knew what to do as if I had practiced for this eventuality. Immediately my mind conjured up a wall of ice, against which the flame licked harmlessly, and I could sense Dagon's snarling as its attack was foiled.

For several rounds, Dagon launched its weapons against me, and I was able to respond. Once it tried an attack against the still insensible Agathe, but I beat it back easily, since I was under no immediate threat and could use all my energy against it. Still, though, I was unable to take the offensive in the struggle.

As I beat off the attacks, I became aware of another presence close at hand. At first I thought it was Agathe regaining consciousness, but a sardonic chuckle soon corrected my misapprehension.

"So you could not keep away, eh, Gauthier?" came the words of Professor Lamartine.

Chapter XXVIII

To say I was surprised to hear his voice is something of an understatement. However, on reflection, I remembered that we had entered the Untime in search of this very man, and it should have been no surprise at all to me to encounter him.

"I perceive you have met Moloch," he said to me.

"I call it Dagon," I replied. I repelled another attack, this one taking the form of a hail of pebbles, against which I erected a shield from which they rebounded harmlessly.

"Moloch, Dagon, Beelzebub. Can you doubt that he and his kind are the origin of the old pagan gods?"

"No doubt in my mind whatsoever," I answered, warding off another shower of stones. I was beginning to be irritated that Lamartine was not assisting me in defending his daughter. However, as soon as I had formulated the thought, I remembered that in the Untime, thoughts are not private.

"What? My Agathe is with you?" came the response. "How dare you bring her into this wilderness? And how did you get here anyway?"

"It was impossible to stop her. We came through the machine in the Vincennes house." Another attack by Dagon, this time in the form of a spray of acid. I quickly coated Agathe and myself with an alkaline solution, including Lamartine for good measure, and the acid hissed and bubbled in a futile manner against this defence. I explained Agathe's situation and her current condition and the dilemma in which I found myself to Lamartine.

"Well, maybe you are not as stupid as I believed you to be. But now, if you will excuse me, I will take Agathe with me and I will return to that house in Vincennes. You may amuse yourself with our friend here." He laughed unpleasantly.

"If that is what you want to do," I said, "pray go ahead. Professor Schneider will be waiting for you there, together with a number of gentlemen from the Gendarmerie, who will be delighted to make your acquaintance in connection with the disappearance of little Marie." I added the gendarmes on the spur of the moment, and it appeared that my invention had an effect on him.

"Schneider, that pompous buffoon? I spit on him. But the gendarmes, ah, that is a different matter. Then I will go elsewhere with Agathe. As you know, anywhere in space and time is possible for one in the Untime."

"First, though, you will have to take Agathe from me," I retorted.

"Why, detaching Agathe from your company should prove a simple matter," he sneered. As he spoke, Dagon shifted its attention from me to the unsuspecting Lamartine, and cast a shower of fiery scorpion-like creatures at him, many of which appeared to strike him, and he winced at their impact.

"It seems to me," I said, being unable to refrain from gloating a little at the discomfiture of my enemy, "that it is you who may have to provide amusement for our friend, while Agathe and I leave the Untime together. Believe me, if you return out of the Untime to our own time, you will find many hands raised against you."

"No!" he fairly shrieked. "You cannot do this to me! We are bound by our common humanity. We, the representatives of *homo sapiens*, must stand together against this hellish monster."

This was a very different tune that he was singing now from the one he had sung only minutes earlier, and I did not hesitate to remind him of the fact, as I used my powers, which were gaining in strength with every one of Dagon's attacks, to deflect a wave of burning oil that threatened to engulf the three of us.

"Very well," he huffed. "I give you my word. You and Agathe will be able to leave the Untime together. I suppose I am correct in assuming that there is some kind of understanding between the two of you?"

The old devil! How could he possibly have known? But I answered as truthfully as I could. "Yes, I love her, and I believe she loves me."

"Then you may have a father's blessing, if that is what you desire. Now let us defeat this beast."

"May I make a suggestion, Professor?" I asked, as a hundred whips, grasped by a hundred tentacles, lashed down upon us, and I quickly raised up a shield to protect us. The attacks were becoming indiscriminate now, not aimed at any one of us, but seemingly expressions of furious anger and rage, directed at our little group as a whole.

"By all means," he gasped.

"I feel confident enough to launch attacks of my own against Dagon, provided that you can hold off the attacks he launches against us. I do not have the strength to defend and attack at the same time."

"I will do my best," said Lamartine, whose confidence and bluster seemed to have evaporated since Dagon's attacks had started to include him as a target.

"Let us work together, then," I told him. Together we beat off a number of assaults from Dagon, of different kinds each time, and Lamartine's defences appeared to be growing in strength and effectiveness at each attack. Though my defences were undeniably stronger, the Professor brought a touch of ingenuity and sophistication to his efforts, which more than compensated for the relative weakness of the defence itself.

"Very well," I said to him after the fifth such attack. "Are you ready to hold off the assault alone, while I go on the attack?"

"I am ready," he said, his voice steady.

I timed my moves carefully. Dagon flashed a mass of flaming swords at us, and Lamartine threw up a corresponding mass of adamantine shields against which the swords clanged harmlessly and the flames extinguished themselves. While this was going on, I conjured up a huge crossbow, similar to the ones used in medieval times in the sieges of castles, and aimed a barbed dart in the general direction of the dark shining eyes visible through the forest of tentacles.

A second or so after the bolt had been loosed, an ear-splitting inhuman scream split the Untime, and

the tentacles which had been holding the swords re-
coiled as if stung.

"Bravo, Gauthier!" exclaimed the Professor. "A few
more of those, and we shall have disposed of this
thing."

"It will be ready for something similar next time," I
reminded him. "I must change tactics."

We waited for the next assault, but Dagon seemed
disinclined to initiate hostilities this time. "It was
hurt worse by the dart than I imagined," I said.

"Alternatively," responded Lamartine, "it is intelligent enough to know that it cannot defend itself and
launch an attack at the same time. It is waiting for us
to attack so that it can defend itself, and having successfully done so, then launch its own attack."

This line of thought seemed plausible to me.
"What do you propose that we do?" I asked him.

"Why, attack, of course," he said. "I will be ready,
should it launch a counter-attack against us."

I prepared my attack, which consisted of fireballs,
and sent the blazing projectiles on their way. Again,
the fearsome scream, and a hail of arrows, but rather than the indiscriminate attacks that Dagon had
been making, these were now all directed solely at
the Professor. His defences were becoming weaker,
and I made a move to assist him.

"No! Go back!" he shouted to me. "Don't you see?
The thing is attempting to pick us off one by one, so
that it may feast at leisure. Go now, and take Agathe
with you. Go! Go, you fool, and save my daughter!"
he screamed, as an arrow pierced his arm.

"I cannot leave you now," I said, but even as I spoke,
I realised the futility of my words, and the correct-
ness of the Professor's analysis of the situation.

"You must leave," he repeated. "Our enemy cannot

leave the Untime unless one of us accompanies him. You go now with Agathe, and leave me here to die. You tell me there is no future for me in Paris. Very well, then. Let my last moments at least serve one whom I love." So saying, he turned to the monster Dagon, and flung a dart of his own into the mass of tentacles.

Again a shriek from Dagon, but there was no respite in the storm of arrows that flew towards the Professor.

I took hold of Agathe, who was still insensible, and took the steps towards the house in Vincennes. Before we stepped out of the Untime, I glanced back. The Professor was lying, still, his body riddled by arrows, and Dagon was moving ever closer to his body, the dark beak snapping in seeming anticipation of the coming feast.

I shuddered, and took another step, which carried me into Vincennes.

Chapter XXIX

T is hard for me to put the events following our return from the Untime into order. Schneider informed me later that when I and Agathe appeared, he assumed that we were corpses. As before, my body was apparently extremely cold, as was that of Agathe, and I had collapsed insensible.

However, on arranging our supposed cadavers in more seemly postures than the ones into which we had fallen, he detected a faint pulse in my wrist, and after holding a mirror up to Agathe's nostrils, detected signs of life in her, also.

According to Schneider, both Agathe and I were unconscious for the best part of twelve hours after our return, during which time, he did not dare to leave the room, let alone the house. However, at length I opened my eyes and looked around me.

On observing that I was awake, Schneider hastened to my side, and gave me some brandy and water, which restored my strength a little.

"How is she?" were my first words, when I had

swallowed a little of the elixir.

"She is still unconscious," he told me. "But she is breathing steadily, and there appears to be no physical damage."

"Thank God!" I breathed, and fell back. Slowly, as I returned to full consciousness, our experiences in the Untime came back to me in all their horror. "Lamartine?" I croaked. "He is not here?"

Schneider shook his head. "No, naturally he is not here," he said, as if humouring an infant. "I was hoping you would be able to inform me of his whereabouts, That, after all, was the reason for you entering the Untime."

Briefly, for I did not wish Agathe to hear all that I had to say about her father, I informed Schneider of what had passed in the Untime, omitting the details of the change in gender, which I had no wish to discuss with anyone at that time. He was fascinated by my account of our visit to Australia, and to Cleopatra's court, but he sucked his teeth when I told him of Dagon, and the battle that had been waged.

"This is one of the matters that I feared Lamartine did not understand well enough," he said. "Heaven knows that this planet with its modest three dimensions holds enough dangers in the form of predatory fauna. We might well expect the Untime to contain monsters beyond our imagination, and who knows what the result might be should they decide to make their home with us?

"Lamartine has perished defending the one he loved," he added. "I can see for myself, Gauthier, that you also love his daughter. I am sure that you had the courage to die for her. Do you have the courage to live for her?"

"Why, what can you mean?" I asked.

"As I mentioned at one time, there is a possibility that one's mental faculties will be permanently impaired as the result of a stay in the Untime. Do you have the courage to stay with her and to maintain her if it transpires that she is in that state, to the end of your days?"

The prospect that he held before me filled me with horror, and it must have showed in my eyes, for Schneider, watching me, nodded slowly. However, a single glance at the prostrate form stretched out on the *chaise longue* was enough . "Of course I will do anything for her," I replied with some heat. "Can you doubt me?"

"No, I cannot say that I would," replied Schneider, "having seen for myself what manner of man you are. But wait..." As he spoke, Agathe's eyelids fluttered, and her hand stole to her brow.

I waited with trepidation to see whether my dear Agathe was indeed the same person who had entered the Untime, or whether she was, as I prayed she was not, impaired and damaged by her sojourn in those mysterious dimensions.

I need not have worried. She opened her eyes, and looked at me. "Jules?" she said in faint tones. "And Professor Schneider? You need not fear for my mental state. I am perfectly in command of all my faculties, even if my physical state is somewhat weak at present."

Schneider and I regarded each other with horror that she had apparently been listening to our conversation. I looked at her enquiringly.

"I was not unconscious at any time," she said to me. "When that monster approached us, my mind was still alert and remained so all the time, though I was unable to communicate, and it soon became obvious that even my unconscious thoughts were not perceptible to those near me. I was conscious of the way in which you so bravely protected me, though, dear Jules, and the way that you and my father fought together to save me, and how my father sacrificed himself—" At this point, her eyes filled with tears, and Schneider, embarrassed, went to her side and offered her his handkerchief, with which she wiped her eyes.

"You need have no worries or regrets, Jules," she assured me. "Naturally, I mourn my father, and am sad that he and you quarrelled in the Untime, but—" Once again, she shook with sobs, but this time I was by her side, and I held her hand and pressed it gently.

"It will pass," she said. "Time will repair what the Untime destroyed."

And so it transpired.

Immediately after Agathe's and my return from the Untime, Professor Schneider was able to inform the world, in an interview that I persuaded old Simon to print in the magazine, that Professor Lamartine had perished in an accident connected with his diving-apparatus at the naval dockyards. For reasons of national security, details were not to be revealed, and his body was unfortunately never recovered. Though this news caused some alarm among the public, and demands for an enquiry into the matter, the affair was never followed up.

Little Marie was never seen again. To the best of my knowledge, the gendarmerie still have her listed as missing. The poor little tot is, as far as I can understand these things, perpetually in the past, in an endless loop in which she ages three years, and then is violently hurled back into the past.

You may express some wonder as to what happened to the apparatus which we used to enter the Untime, both at Lamartine's laboratory and at the Vincennes house. When Agathe and I had fully recovered from the physical effects of the Untime, which took about one month, she and I met Professor Schneider, to discuss what should be done with Lamartine's inventions. Schneider had persuaded the owner of the Vincennes property to let it to him, without any further work being done to it, so we had no concerns about the machinery being tampered with or misused. There was also the machinery at the Lamartine laboratories to be considered.

Though both Agathe and I had experience of the Untime, and we could both could perceive its value as a tool to be used for historical research, and also of its convenience as regards instant travel, we both decided, with Schneider's reluctant agreement, that the risks involved in maintaining these links to the Untime were too great, and the possibilities for abuse by unscrupulous parties were too tempting.

Accordingly, Schneider and I personally dismantled both sets of apparatus, and sold the parts as scrap metal. Agathe went through her father's writings, and extracted any which appeared to be concerned with the Untime, which we then burned. Though Agathe was stricken with grief at the death of her father, she came to the realisation, after looking through the papers that she discovered in the laboratory, that his great mind had for some time been slipping away from the paths of reason. Though he was capable enough in so many ways, his thoughts and energies when outside the scientific sphere appeared to be more than a little irrational.

Professor Schneider, to whom she showed the papers on which she based her discovery, concurred. To him, it seemed that over-exposure to the quick-silver which was employed in the Untime apparatus could well have caused Lamartine's mind to become unhinged, to put it bluntly, and gave me his confidential opinion that if the degeneration of his faculties had continued, there would have been no alternative but to place the distinguished professor into the care of an asylum for the insane.

As tactfully as I was able, I conveyed these opinions to Agathe, who was aghast at the news, and fell into a fresh paroxysm of grief from which it took her some considerable time to recover.

During this period of grief, she and I talked at length about our experiences in the Untime, and it was clear to both of us that the bond that had been forged between us there was one that would never be broken. I proposed marriage to this remarkable woman, and to my everlasting joy, she accepted me without reservation. The thought of a future happy life together with me, I may say with all due modesty, was one of those factors that brought Agathe from the shadow of grief back to the land of the living.

Six months after our return from the Untime, Agathe and I were married, and Professor Schneider acted as our best man.

True to his word, Schneider found Agathe a place at the University, where she conducts research into matters beyond my poor understanding, and has won herself a name among those who are conversant in these matters.

But whatever else she may be, she remains my faithful and loving companion, with whom I can never forget that we once shared the excitement and the perils of the Untime.

About
Inknbeans Press

INKNBEANS PRESS is all about the ultimate reading experience. We believe books are the greatest treasures of mankind. In them are held all the history, fantasy, hope and horror of humanity. We can experience the past, dream of the future, understand how everything works from an atomic clock to the human heart. We can explore our souls, fight epic battles, swoon in love. We can fly, we can run, we can cross mighty oceans and endless universes. We can invite ancient cultures into our living room, and walk on the moon. And if we can do it with a decent cup of coffee beside us...well, what more can we ask, right?

Visit the Web site at www.inknbeans.com

More from
Inknbeans Press

When Clouds Touch:
Ey Wade

Ey Wade's *When Clouds Touch* is the embodiment of a story of soulmates, Paisley and Malachi.

Destined to meet since before birth, their story wraps us somewhere between loving and caring, wanting the best for someone, while wanting to see them happy, even when it is risky and they must obey the demands of family.

Paisley, a woman of Japanese descent, living with Albinism and heart disease, is meek, yet makes no apologies for seeking what she yearns. Hiding behind the protective fold of her *wagasa*, she yearns for freedom from her overprotective parents and the love of a man she's known only in her dreams, even at the cost of her health.

Malachi, a man who has visions of meeting an elusive shadow, uses his sense of humour and sensitive side to build their relationship. He's determined to win her love, even against the wishes of her parents.

THE VORTEX ENTRANCE – BOOK 1 OF THE DISAPPEARING SERIES: JACKSON HORVAT

FOURTEEN YEAR OLD JOHN WEAVER; A normal teenager, entering yet another new school. After his Mom makes him and his little sister move for what seems like the millionth time, John's about tired of the stress that each new school brings. She claims it's for new scenery, but John knows what she's really trying to escape.

His dad. He left when John was just a toddler, and he can barely even remember him.

At least there's his friend Dominic, who's simply moved with them every time. Maybe their moms like to keep in touch, John's never quite sure. That's the only relief. John's whole first day is awful, but then something happens.

Something . . . strange.

John's life is thrown upside down. Everything he's ever known is basically a lie. And then his mom . . . his mom's taken from him.

His whole world that he knew is ripped from beneath him and he's forced into a strange, and frightening life. A dangerous life. A life where people are powerful. A life where people can kill.

A life where a war is brewing . . .

Letting Go:
Andy Boerger

A LITTLE PILOT.
A big problem.
A story for anyone who has ever lost, and then found, his wings.

ANDY BOERGER is also the author and illustrator of *I Like you More Each Day*, the story of little Meg and her wise ferret, as well as providing the delightful illustrations for the series of Sherlock Ferret children's books written by Hugh Ashton.